THE CHICKEN BURGER MURDER

A Burger Bar Mystery Book 3

ROSIE A. POINT

Copyright Rosie A. Point 2019.

Join my no-spam newsletter and receive an exclusive offer. Details can be found at the back of this book.

Cover by DLR Cover Designs
www.dlrcoverdesigns.com

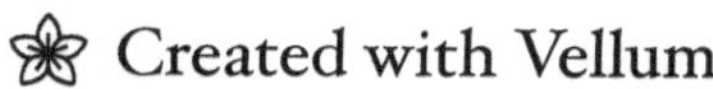 Created with Vellum

YOU'RE INVITED!

Hi there, reader!

I'd like to formally invite you to join my awesome community of readers. We love to chat about cozy mysteries, cooking, and pets.

It's super fun because I get to share chapters from yet-to-be-released books, fun recipes, pictures, and do giveaways with the people who enjoy my stories the most.

So whether you're a new reader or you've been

enjoying my stories for a while, you can catch up with other like-minded readers, and get lots of cool content by visiting my website at *www.rosiepointbooks.com* and signing up for my mailing list.

Or simply search for me on *www.bookbub.com* and follow me there.

I look forward to getting to know you better.

Let's get into the story!

Yours,
Rosie

❧ I ❧

The mayor of Sleepy Creek stood on the podium in the town hall, his gavel in one hand, and his fist on his hip. "Now," he said, to the waiting citizens. "Now, now, everyone quiet down."

I sat at the back of the hall—best vantage point in the place—with Grizzy practically squirming at my side. "Relax," I said. "You'd swear it was Christmas tomorrow."

"Shush, shush, it's going to start soon."

"Perish the thought we would miss a single second of Mayor Samson's riveting speech."

Missi, who had taken her place in front of me next to her twin sister, Virginia, snorted loudly. She shared my enthusiasm for these town meetings, but then, the terrible twins had attended every single one since they'd been eighteen-years-old. They were nigh on eighty now.

"Settle down, everyone," the mayor called, clearing his throat. He brought his gavel down on the wooden stand, and the clacking rose above the general shuffling and chatter in the hall.

"I don't get why everyone's so excited about this," I whispered. "It's not like..."

"Shush." Grizzy insisted.

I pressed my fingers to the bridge of my nose. It had been a week since the last murder in Sleepy Creek, and, after all that high octane investigation, things had slowed down a lot. It was a good thing—I'd received my final warning from the Chief back in Boston.

One more hint of trouble and my sabbatical would be over. So would my future as a homicide detective in Boston. But quiet was... boring. Unless I counted the incident with Maura's cat, and the run-in with the blender I'd had the other morning—I couldn't be held liable for spraying smoothie all over the ceiling. I'd been tired.

"All right, now that you're all settled," the mayor prompted, over the last few whispers. "I'm proud to announce that we'll be holding the Spring Food Fair as planned this year."

The announcement was greeted with thunderous applause. A few of the locals stamped their feet on the wooden boards.

"Before we get into the details of our fair," the mayor continued, raising his palm. "I would like for us to take a moment of silence to pay homage to those we've lost this past month. To Paul and to Haley. May they rest in peace."

Everyone bowed their heads and fell silent.

I couldn't think about Haley or Paul. Doing so excited my investigative brain, and that would only lead to trouble. After all,

Paul's death might have been linked to my mother's cold case.

Instead, I fixed my gaze on the mayor.

He was tall and broad-shouldered, but his belly strained against the buttons of his plaid shirt. He was in his late sixties with graying hair and a slightly bulbous nose. I didn't know him well, but the rumors in the Burger Bar said he was a good man. The most trusted in the town, according to Vee. Missi grew all prune-lipped at the mention of the man.

Perhaps, because he was the guy in Sleepy Creek who had the most power. Or he'd inadvertently insulted her. An argument over an antique? Anything was possible when it came to Missi.

She was the one who'd suggested I get a cat solely for the purpose of human body disposal.

"Thank you," the mayor said. "Now, I know this has been a difficult time for everyone, and that there were some in the town who thought having the Food Fair this year might be in bad taste. But Sleepy Creek is nothing without its traditions, and this is one we must continue at all costs."

"Hear, hear," a man near the front called out. "Can't let a few murders stop our celebration, am I right?" He was so tall he was a head and shoulders above everyone else sitting down, with olive skin and dark hair—balding spot in the center of his head.

"Who's that?" I whispered.

"Sal from the pizzeria," Grizzy replied.

I hadn't met the owner of the pizzeria, but their fully stacked pepperoni was just about the best pie I'd had in my life.

"Now, Sal, let's try to be respectful," the mayor said, and smiled kindly.

"Whatever, Samson, get to the good stuff."

The mayor didn't look pleased. "Right," he said, "you'll notice that there's a fair ground map underneath each of your chairs. I'll ask you to remove it, now."

"This is like Oprah without the cars," I whispered.

Missi snorted again.

I brought out the map, and the other citizens did too. It was a schematic of the park in the center of Sleepy Creek with plots mapped out around the fountain. The ones closest to the winding path that tracked across the grass would likely get the most attention.

Each plot was numbered.

"As you can see, we've got our layout ready for the Food Fair," the mayor said. "Last year, we had some difficulty selecting which stall would go where."

A few of the others grumbled, and I raised an eyebrow at Grizzy.

"Infighting," she whispered.

"—we're going to streamline the selection process this year." The mayor brought out a large clear plastic bowl. "Inside, there are numbers. Each person gets to pick one."

"Do you really think that's fair?" Sal sprang from his seat. "What if none of the food stalls get a front row position?"

"Oh please." A woman stood. Mid-forties,

by my estimation, with fiery red hair. Short, but stocky, looked as if she'd pack a punch. "You want the best stall spot for yourself. Don't think I've forgotten about last year."

"What about last year?" Sal asked, in an accent that smacked of New York.

"You got the best stall for yourself and the rest of us were left in the second row, far away from the fountain. At least, this way is fair."

"Dolores, if the cakes don't sell, get out of the bakery. That's what I always say." Sal clicked his fingers and pointed at her.

"Oh, you are a horrible man. Horrible, horrible man. Selfish! You want all the money for yourself."

"Now, now, you two, relax," the mayor said, and banged his gavel on the stand.

But the two glared at each other. It didn't seem that either of them would back down.

"You want it all for yourself," Dolores repeated.

"Like I said, Dolores, if nobody's buying

your product there's got to be a reason for it. From what I hear, stale goods."

"How dare you!"

A few people gasped.

The mayor brought his gavel down twice. "That's enough."

"I'm not the one who serves stinky cheese on his pizzas," Dolores said.

"Keep talking." Sal made a quacking motion with one hand. "Keep talking. It's music to my ears."

"Both of you sit down, immediately. If you don't behave, neither of you will pick until last."

That shut them up fast. They lowered themselves into their seats again, Sal with sniff, and Dolores with a huff and a puff and a straightening of her polka dot cardigan.

"As if we haven't had enough drama in Sleepy Creek," Virginia said, turning her head to catch my eye. "Those two have been at each other's throats for years. Each Spring Food Fair it's the same. Arguments. Tears, mostly from Sal, and the comparison of sales at the end of the charity drive."

"They're idiots," Missi grunted.

"Be nice." Her plum-haired sister tapped her on the forearm.

"No," Missi said, "and you can't make me either."

I grinned. The twins always cheered me up, even when I was the butt of their joke—it happened more often that I liked to admit.

The mayor had descended from the podium with his bowl and started in the front row. He walked up and down the lines, waiting as people drew their numbers. Chatter started as people compared their stall positions. Dolores had a look on her face like she'd bitten into a rotten apple. She glanced over at Sal, and drew her tongue over her bottom lip.

"Here you are, Griselda." Samson held out the bowl, and my bestie reached into it and withdrew a slip of paper. The mayor moved on down the line.

"What did you get?" I asked.

"Number 13."

"Way to give me the creeps."

"It's spring not Halloween, Chris."

"I was kidding." I drew the map out and pointed to the number. "Nice! That's right next to the path, across from the fountain."

"Wow," Grizzy said. "That's the best spot I've ever gotten. I can't wait for the fair now."

"Don't let Sal or Dolores hear about it." Missi had turned around in her chair. "They'll try to steal the paper from you. Or sabotage your burgers."

"For real?" I asked.

"Of course." Missi's answer was matter-of-fact. "Those two will do anything to get what they want. Haven't you heard about the cake-pizza war of 2016?"

"No. Not sure I want to. Was it like a massive food fight?"

"Basically," Missi said. "But with guerrilla tactics. Went on for months. Cakes plastered against the pizzeria, loads of ants, and then the stench of cheese outside the bakery. Took that handsome detective you're in love with to stop it."

I choked on saliva. "What?"

"The stench of cheese?" Missi asked, innocently.

"I am not in love with Detective Balle," I snapped.

"Funny," Missi replied, a twinkle in her sharp blue eyes. "I didn't mention his name."

I rolled my eyes and sat back as the mayor resumed his spot on the podium. If Missi was in such good spirits because of the Food Fair, she'd be insufferable for the rest of the week. Assuming no one else in Sleepy Creek got murdered.

❧ 2 ❧

"It's this way," I said, gesturing with the map of the park. "Should be right across from the fountain?"

"This is too exciting." Grizzy carried our takeaway containers from the Burger Bar, one stacked on top of the other, grinning. "I can't believe we got such a great spot for the Fair. Last year, I was two rows from the front."

"I'm sure you sold a ton of burgers. Who could resist them?" I walked next to my friend, down the long winding path that led through the park, under trees and past the odd pond or bench. The scent of new flowers was on the air, and I inhaled deeply.

"A ton of burgers? Maybe. OK, yeah, we did sell a lot, but still. This will give us even more visibility." Grizzy kept up the pace, bouncing along out of sheer excitement. "Sleepy Creek's becoming more popular, you know."

"Meaning what?"

"The tourism season is just starting. Old Belle at the Sleepy Dreams Guesthouse is already fully booked up, and so is the Sleepy Creek motel. This will draw in a lot of new customers and get people talking about the Burger Bar." Grizzy bit her lip. "I've been thinking ... I mean, after the twins set up their social media page, maybe I should put one up too. And a website."

I nearly tripped over my feet, the map of the park slipping in my fingers. I caught it before it fell. "You don't have a website?"

"That was a bit of an overreaction. It's not

like I just announced I don't have an aortic valve."

I raised an eyebrow at her.

"What? I've been watching a lot of those ask the doctor type shows on TV."

"I beg you to stop."

"My point," Grizzy said, "is that I'm thinking, if I put a website up I'll draw in even more customers."

"Build hype for the Fair?"

"Not just that, but for the tourism season in general. Can you imagine? People traveling from all over to come taste our burgers."

"Ah, here it is." I gestured to a patch of grass across from the fountain. A bench sat to the left of what would be the Burger Bar's lot, though it hadn't been demarcated yet.

"It's perfect." Grizzy sighed and lowered herself to the bench.

"To be fair, it's just a patch of grass."

"It's a patch of potential."

I sat next to Grizzy, and she handed me

one of the takeaway burger boxes, smiling almost from ear-to-ear.

"What are you so happy about?" I asked.

"Well, what did we come here for today?"

"Fresh air? Sunshine? An opportunity to get sprayed by the fountain? Make a wish in the waters? To burn some calories after the last week of—"

"I don't know why I ask you questions. You've always got something spunky to say."

"You like that about me, though."

Grizzy chuckled. "In moderation."

"Hashtag mean."

"Oh, don't start hash-tagging things. You know I don't understand how it works."

"Good heavens, Griselda, even Virginia knows how hash-tagging works and she's nearly eighty."

Grizzy popped open the box on her lap then handed me one of the napkins from underneath it. "My point is," she said, "that we came to figure out what type of burgers we should serve at the Fair. Now, Jarvis is happy to do any of them, but he did give me a quick list of what he wouldn't like to do."

"And they are?"

"He doesn't want to do anything with eggs because that might be more difficult in large quantities," Griz said.

"Makes sense." I opened by burger box and removed the delicious item.

"And he thinks the Double Cheese Burger will probably take too much time to get right on the day. So, he came up with a solution. Take a bite."

I bit into the burger, and the burst of flavor traveled over my tongue. The textures were unbelievable too. The crunch of deep fried crumbing, the softness of tender chicken breasts, the crispiness of lettuce. The buns were perfect as always, light, with sesame seeds on the top, and toasted on the inside so the burger would maintain its integrity.

"Oh wow," I said, around a mouthful. "It's chicken."

"Exactly," Griz replied. "Nothing fancy.

The humble Chicken Burger will be our little surprise for the residents of Sleepy Creek and the visitors. Jarvis thinks he can pull it off easily. And I've got a supplier—"

A shout rang out nearby, and Grizzy paused, frowning. I scanned the park and spotted two people standing on the trail to the left of the fountain, facing each other.

Sal wearing a marinara stained apron with Sal's Pizzeria logo on the front, and…

"Is that Nelly? From the florists' shop?" Grizzy placed her hand over her eyes. "What on Earth?"

Nelly had her fists on her hips. She glared up at Sal, anger burning in her usually mellow face. I hadn't lived in Sleepy Creek for long now—just the three weeks since I'd been placed on sabbatical—but I'd never once seen Nelly angry.

She was usually pleasant. She hated conflict and gossip and anything negative.

"I won't," she said, loudly, and walked off.

Sal followed her. "Hey, I'm talkin' to you."

"I don't want to hear anything you have to say, Sal."

"Uh oh," Grizzy said, and put her burger back in its box

I did the same and shut the lid to protect it from an incursion of flies or bugs. I'd never been a big fan of eating stuff outdoors. "What do you think that's about?"

"My gut instinct says it's got something to do with the Fair."

Nelly and Sal were closer, now, drawing even with our bench. Nelly spotted us and tried to dismiss Sal by coming over. But the owner of the pizzeria didn't take the hint. He trailed after her.

"Morning," Nelly said, her cheeks pink. "Are you two doing well? Out for a lunch break in the park?"

"Yes, Martin's taking care of—"

"I know what you're doing here," Sal spoke over Grizzy. "Scoping out your spot for the Fair, eh? You probably think you've won just because you got a prime spot, but it won't be easy. Your food has to be good to make sales."

"I wouldn't insult her, if I were you," I said, coolly. "Or talk over her for that matter."

"And why's that?" Sal cocked his head to one side. "You think I'm afraid of you, little woman?"

What a detestable man. "No, but I do think you're the type of man who doesn't want to run afoul of the law."

"Christie's a detective." Nelly raised her chin.

Sal shut his thick lips, but they wriggled, as if he had to force himself not to say anything else. "Whatever," he grumbled. "I didn't come to talk to you, anyway, Griselda. You and your burgers are a waste of my time." He stomped off down the path and out of sight.

We watched him go in silence, and I shook my head. "What was that about?"

"I have no idea. That's the first time Sal's ever insulted me. We usually get on pretty well," Griz said. "We're not exactly in competition. I mean, people either like pizza or they like burgers or they alternate."

"He's angry," Nelly said, dragging her fingers through her mousy brown hair, "because I got a spot in front of the fountain and he didn't. He said that I have no right to be selling flowers at the front. That it should only be food stalls along the main path, and that I should give up my spot to him. That it was the right thing to do."

"Oh, Nelly, I hope you refused," Grizzy replied. "That's not fair of him."

"Of course I said no. That man is as stubborn as a mule, though. He kept following me. I mean, you saw..." she let out a frustrated grunt. "I don't like arguing with people. Why can't he leave me alone?"

"Sounds like Sal's got an ego problem. Or maybe it's a financial problem?" I tapped my chin.

"No, no, no, don't you dare, Watson." Grizzy poked me on the shoulder.

"Dare what?"

"You're tapping your chin again. That's your 'I'm about to get involved' tell. Sal's issues are not yours to solve."

"Fine, fine," I said, and lifted my hands. "I just think it's interesting that he's so eager for a front spot. What difference does it make?"

"It's hotly contested," Nelly said. "They are prime spots. I just think it's rude. I mean, half of the proceeds do go to charity. It doesn't seem in keeping with the spirit of the Fair." She readjusted her beige sweater. "Anyway, I'd better get back to the shop."

"Take care, Nelly," Grizzy said.

After the florist had left, we sat in silence eating our chicken burgers. My thoughts wandered from Sal's strange behavior, to Sleepy Creek, to the Fair, and, finally, to my mother's cold case. It was a cycle I was accustomed to.

Now that it was quiet in the town, free of murders and cases to investigate, thank goodness, I had nothing much else to fixate on. Hopefully, it stayed that way.

❧ 3 ❧

"Ready to go?" Griz asked, from behind the counter in the Burger Bar.

It was a sunny Friday morning and uncommonly warm outside. Every customer who'd come through the doors had commented on it, and the sales of milkshakes and soda floats were higher than they'd been in two weeks.

The mood in the restaurant brought happiness to me that I hadn't experienced in longer than I cared to admit. It gave me all kinds of questions—why was I happy now, when all I'd ever wanted was to be a homicide detective and find the truth? And if I was happier here than back in Boston, did that mean I would be unhappy when my sabbatical finally ended?

I spun my tray on the tip of my finger, absently.

"Christie?"

"Hmm?"

"Are you ready to go?" Griz lifted a cardboard box, packed with takeaway boxes, and set it down on the counter. "We don't want to be late. Mayor Samson is a stickler for punctuality."

"And for wearing plaid shirts," I replied, and picked up the box. We were due at the town hall today to provide the Mayor and the appointed Food Fair council with tasters of what we'd be selling.

"What's wrong with plaid shirts?" Griz asked.

"Nothing. It's just ... there are other colors, you know." We waved to Martin on our way out, and the hero of the restaurant gave us a thumbs up back.

I carried the box down the street, the sun warming my face, and Grizzy humming at my side. "I love spring," she said. "It's not too hot, not too cold, most of the time, and the smell of the flowers is on the air." She drew in a deep breath.

"And burgers," I replied. "And pizza. Especially with the Food Fair coming up."

"Yeah, that's a bonus. And it's nice that we'll be able to give something back too. Two years ago, the Fair didn't even sponsor a charity."

"Really?"

"Yeah," Grizzy said, as we turned the corner and moved past glass windows, wrought iron lamps and storefronts. "It was actually Dolores' suggestion that we give half of the proceeds to a charity of the town's choice. Naturally, Sal was furious about that."

"He was?"

"Yes, but I think it was more because it

was Dolores who suggested it. After that there was a resurgence in pizza and cake warfare."

"This place is something else," I said.

We fell silent, and I mulled over the morning, the upcoming fair, and tried my best to resist the scent of the burgers rising from the containers. My stomach growled. I had been holding off on snacking on burgers because it had been less than a month and I'd already packed on a few pounds.

The stress of investigating under the radar hadn't burned enough calories to keep me slim. And Jarvis did love to go heavy on the cheese.

We arrived at the town hall and entered to find the place packed with people and tables already arrayed with tasty bites. There were slices of Sal's pizza in the far corner of the room, and Dolores had stacked her cupcakes in neat little boxes with clear tops. The two cast glares at each other between the crowds of townsfolk.

"Let's set up here," Griz said.

I followed her over to one of the empty spaces at a table far enough from Dolores and Sal to avoid the 'heat in the kitchen.' The hall filled up quite quickly, folks coming with food or to try it. The mayor and the other Food Fair committee members roved through the crowd, stopping to taste samples as they went.

They started near the walnut doors, which had been thrown wide open, and worked their way clockwise around the hall. The chatter was loud and merry and the smells delicious.

"Good morning, Griselda," Mayor Samson said, stopping in front of our section on one of the tables. "And good morning, Christie."

"Hi," we said, in unison.

"What have you got for us to sample to-day?" he asked.

The other committee members gathered as well, smiling amiably at the boxes.

Griselda lifted one of the boxes and opened it. "I present to you, the humble Chicken Burger."

A collection of 'ooh's' and 'ahs' traveled through the group, and some of the others in the hall gathered round to take a peek.

"We've cut them into quarters so that it's easier for everyone to taste test," I said, and began opening the other takeaway boxes.

The committee members nudged in closer, bumping elbows, some of them licking their lips. They tried the food and chewed enthusiastically, nodding.

"This is fantastic," Mayor Samson said, and accepted a napkin from Grizzy. "And you think you'll be able to prepare these with ease?"

"Jarvis is set, and I'll be helping him along. Christie and Martin too. We're all hands on deck for the Food Fair."

Now, I wasn't one for Fairs or crowds, but this was kind of fun. The vibe in the hall was warm and friendly, and I'd grown accustomed to the Sleepy Creek credo over the past few weeks—gossip, food, and oddities.

"Fantastic," the mayor said. "Well, that's settled then. I think we'll—"

A shout followed by gasps and the stamp of feet interrupted him. The crowd further back in the hall pushed and shoved, and a few people cried out for help.

"What's going on there?" Mayor Samson raised his voice. "Settle down, settle down. Excuse me, ladies." He bustled off with his committee members in tow.

"What do you think that's about?" Grizzy asked.

"Only one way to find out." My curiosity peaked. I stepped out from behind the trestle table and squeezed past members of the crowd. Finally, I burst out into a small clearing in the corner of the hall, right next to Sal's table of pizza slices.

The mayor stood a few feet from it, his jaw dropped. One of the committee members had fainted, and was being held upright by the man behind her. The people jostling next to me and behind were pale, their eyes wide.

I didn't blame them.

Sal from the pizzeria lay face down on the floor. Head turned to the left. Eyes closed. Piece of pizza lying next to him. Had he passed out? Or was it something worse than that?

"Someone do something!" A yell from the crowd.

I rushed forward and pressed my fingers to the side of his neck. "No pulse," I whispered.

"Someone call an ambulance!" a man shouted further back.

But it was already too late for that.

The jury was out on whether it was murder, but I wasn't about to take my chances hanging around next to his body. I backed up a few steps and rejoined the crowd, shaking my head. The crowd pushed and shoved to get to the front, and I slipped back in among them.

Already, those truth-seeking urges rose inside me.

Had Sal been killed? Poisoned like Haley had been? Was he connected to...?

"Chris?" Grizzy took hold of my forearm. She guided me back to the table and the empty burger boxes. "What happened? What's going on?"

I focused my attention on her.

"What? Goodness, you look crazed. Your eyes are as big as … burger buns."

I blinked.

"And you didn't even tease me for using 'burger buns' as a simile."

"Metaphor," I muttered. "No, simile. I don't care."

"What happened?"

"Sal's dead," I replied, as a siren whooped in the street outside.

Once again, Sleepy Creek was about to become a lot less sleepy and a lot more suspicious.

4

The Burger Bar was abuzz with the news of Sal's passing the next day. The questions, comments and intrigue lasted through the morning burger rush to brunch, when a lot of folks had already headed off to work. Or to share more gossip stories with their book clubs or knitting circles.

I'd done what I could to insulate myself from the rumors—that way I could keep my head out of investigating the death of Sal the pizzeria man. Problem was, most of the folks in Sleepy Creek didn't care what I wanted.

"Information is made to be shared," Missi said, from her favorite spot in the Burger Bar —the corner booth.

Her sister, Virginia, sat across from her and fluffed her plum-gray hair. "She's right, you know. Made to be shared."

"Sounds like an excuse for gossip," I said, as I placed their milkshake orders, one double thick choc and one vanilla, on the table in front of them.

"And what's wrong with that?" Vee asked. "When it's for a good cause, of course." She plucked her cherry off the dollop of cream on top of the milkshake and inserted it between her lips. She crunched on it.

"I know your game," I said. "You want me to get involved, and you know I can't get involved."

"Oh, she does think she's special," Missi clucked. "What makes you think we're interested in you investigating Sal's untimely, and slightly welcome, demise?"

"You asked me to do it for the last murder." I glanced over my shoulder to check my other tables were fine. Things had quieted down in the restaurant, and the customers left were preoccupied with their burgers. Chicken was the flavor of the day.

"Hmmm." Vee tapped her chin. "She has a point."

"Sit down, Watson. You're giving me a neck ache."

"I should get back to—"

"Sit," Missi hissed.

I cast a final glance in Grizzy's direction— she was glued to her cellphone behind the bar, not literally but she might as well have been with that grin on her face.

"Fine." I sank into the chair next to Virginia and placed my tray on the tabletop. "But I'm not going to do any investigating on this one. From what I heard, Sal wasn't murdered."

"From what you heard? Now, who's been gossiping?" Missi smirked.

"I wasn't gossiping. I overheard it."

"Hmm, overheard or eavesdropped?" Vee asked.

"Bit of both. My curiosity got the better of me," I said, and threw caution to the wind. "It's weird, don't you think?"

"That he died?" Missi asked. "Not really. He was incredibly unhealthy. General consensus on the street is that Sal ate so much cheese he was pretty much half-cheese himself. My humble prediction was that he'd throw himself at the front of Dolores' bakery during the next uprising of the pizza versus the cake."

"There's a pleasant image."

"She's right." Vee slurped on her vanilla milkshake. "The man could eat. And that's saying something in this town. Cholesterol problems."

I'd heard much the same during the morning of serving burgers and batting away prying questions about what I'd seen in the town hall. "Cholesterol problems. What a way to go."

"I heard he died right after taking a bite of his own pizza," Missi said. "Apparently, he got tired of waiting for the committee to come over to his stand and helped himself. Total glutton."

"Missi, dear, it's not in good form to speak ill of the dead."

"Oh please, Virginia. He's down there talking ill of all of us, right now. Mark my words."

"Down there?" I grimaced. "He wasn't that bad, was he?"

"He tried to kill Maura's cats. And he liked throwing food around. And he was very grumpy," Missi said.

"You know, you're at least one of those things." I shifted my tray. "Tell you the truth, I'm kinda glad that this isn't a murder investigation."

"Because you have the compulsive need to investigate?" Vee asked.

"She can't help sticking her nose where it doesn't belong."

"That's rich coming from you two," I said. "If it wasn't for my nose, your antique store would be closed, right now."

Missi grunted. "Ever the humble one."

I'd always stick up for myself when backed into a corner. Even if I was backed into a corner by Missi, who happened to be old, harmless and absolutely terrifying all wrapped into one. I'd been on homicide investigations that had involved the mob back in Boston and even those hadn't given me the chills like a stare from Missi did. She reminded me of my school teacher from the first grade.

"Well," I said, "if you've got no other gossip—"

"Wisdom." Missi glared.

"—gossip to impart, then I'll get back to waiting tables and keeping my nose out of Sal's death."

"Always better to protect the nose whenever Sal's involved." Missi nodded.

I slipped out of the booth, collected my tray, and headed back to the counter. Grizzy whistled under her breath and didn't pay me any mind as I approached.

"Talking to your boyfriend?" I asked.

Her head snapped up. "He's not my boyfriend! He's just... Arthur's a friend."

"A friend you go on dates with and talk to all the time. Sure, just a friend." I grinned at her. For all my teasing, I was pretty happy that Griz finally had someone to spend time with other than her slightly overweight cat, Curly Fries. Or me.

I held no delusions about how entertaining I was. I mostly stuck to myself, read books when I wasn't going off to 'stick my nose where it didn't belong,' and I'd never been a people person. Thankfully, Griz accepted me for who I was.

"What did the twins have to say?" Grizzy asked.

"Oh the usual. Doom, gloom and milkshakes."

"I supposed they're curious about what happened to Sal?"

"Everyone's curious about what happened to Sal," I said, and leaned my forearms on the table. "But it looks like my services won't be needed this time around."

"Isn't that a relief?" Griz asked.

"I suppose." It gave me more time to mentally reprimand myself for not trying to find out what had happened with my mother's cold case. I both wanted to investigate and was wary of doing so. If one case would draw me into the deep end, it was that one. Once I had started, I wouldn't stop until I found the answers I needed. And if someone got in the way ... well, it wouldn't matter who it was. I'd steamroll whatever obstacles stood in my path.

The bell above the glass front door tinkled, and I switched my gaze to the mirror.

Dolores the baker entered the Burger Bar,

her fiery red hair loose at her shoulders. She wore a polka dot dress with a striped cardigan —a jarring effect—and grinned around the restaurant. "Lovely morning isn't it?" she said, loudly, and hummed her way over to the bar.

She parked her behind on one of the puffy stools and tapped her fingers on the countertop. "Hello, Griselda, darling. And there you are, Christie."

"You know my name?" I'd only bought a croissant from her once before.

"Of course I do," she said, and tipped two fingers to her forehead in a salute. "You're the detective from Boston. You like croissants with chocolate dipping sauce. I never forget an order or a face."

"How are you this morning, Dolores?" Grizzy asked. "Anything special I can get for you?"

"How am I?" Dolores asked. "How am I? I've never been better! Never been better."

"Why's that?" I had an inkling as to why, but this attitude intrigued me. I wasn't exactly besties with the baker, but the last time I'd seen her in the town hall, she hadn't been this chipper.

"Because spring has sprung, it's a beautiful day, and I am officially free of that horrible, terrible, no good human being, Sal Russo. He's gone. He's dead. He's never going to bother me again."

"You two really didn't get along."

"Understatement of all eternity," she said. "I hated the man. Hated him. And I'm sure it's very sad that he died of coronary heart disease or cheese for blood for some people, at least, but for me, it's like a new dawn."

"He gave you that much trouble?"

Dolores inhaled through her nostrils. "He once shoved an entire slice of pizza up the exhaust pipe of my new delivery van."

"Wow."

"And now, he's gone. Griselda, I'll take a Chicken Burger with all the toppings, please. I can't wait to try out your treat for the Fair this coming weekend. It'll taste so much better knowing that I'll have the stall right across from yours. Customers can stop at your stall, then head to mine for dessert."

"You got the lot across from ours?" I asked, as Griz headed toward the kitchen window to deliver the order to Jarvis.

"Now, I have it. I went to see the mayor this morning, and I managed to snag Sal's lot," she said, and gave a triumphant laugh.

I kept my expression blank, collected my tray, and walked off to serve my tables instead of commenting further. The suspicion had gathered in my gut, along with the question: what if this wasn't a case of too much cheese? What if Sal had been murdered after all?

If so, I already had my prime suspect.

Behind me, Dolores gave a cackle that would have suited a witch.

5

Curly Fries was terrible company at the best of times. She had a penchant for lashing out with scratches and bites when I got too close, and would try stealing food from the kitchen when no one was looking. I suspected she might have found another food provider somewhere in the neighborhood, since she hadn't stopped gaining weight, even though we'd put her on a diet and started taking her for obligatory walks.

But her worst habit, by far, was the staring.

Every single time I sat down to read one of my mystery adventures, or watched a show on TV, or even did a little research on a case, she was *there*. Watching. Waiting. Biding her time until the night, when I'd fall asleep, only to wake up with her lying across my forehead.

Either the black cat liked me and had a terrible way of showing it, or had decided it was her mission in life to punish me for daring to enter Griselda's home.

I lowered my paperback and spied her over the edge of it.

She sat upright on my too-pink comforter, her yellow eyes focused on me, her pupils large.

"Stop it," I said. "You're going to ruin my night." This was the first chance I'd had to tuck into one of my favorite books, another Agatha Christie, in days.

There had been the murder last week, and then there had been work, now the Spring Food Fair coming up, and, when were weren't busy with those things, Griz and I would hang out or chat or watch TV.

Tonight, Griz was preoccupied with Mr. Arthur Cotton. The two had a pizza and movie date in the living room downstairs that Grizzy insisted was *not* a date. She got all flustered whenever I mentioned it.

I tried bowing my head and returning to my book, but Curly Fries flicked her tail and gave a *prrt-meow*.

"What?" I asked. "Is it food again?"

Another flick of the tail.

"You know I can't give you food, Curly." I checked my watch. The pizza was due in a few minutes—Griz had insisted that I order a pie too, so I wouldn't be left out. I'd have to guard the pizza from Curly with my life.

Another meow, this one more indignant than the last, and Curly Fries pranced across the bed and planted her furry butt on my pillow.

"Really?" I asked.

She kept staring. It was impossible to concentrate like this. It was bad enough that Missi and Vee had planted the seeds of doubt in my mind this afternoon—Sal's death had been a fixture in my thoughts since then.

Weirdly, it was part of the reason I'd offered to call the pizzeria tonight. Sal's was still open—the news around Sleepy Creek was that his long-lost cousin had decided to run his restaurant for the next week or two, in his honor.

An intriguing thing to do. Surely, the family would want some time to grieve? Why keep the pizza place open?

The doorbell rang, and I heaved a sigh, put my bookmark between the age-yellowed pages of my paperback, and rose from the bed.

I headed downstairs. "I'll get it," I called out, so Grizzy wouldn't have to interrupt her date by paying for pizza.

"Are you sure?" Griz yelled back. "I can—oh."

I entered the living room from the kitchen and grinned at her. She was seated next to

Arthur on the sofa that faced the TV looking mighty uncomfortable.

"Having fun?" I asked, and winked at her.

Arthur, whose blond hair was slick with gel, cleared his throat and shifted his arm on the back of the sofa. He'd clearly been trying to put it around Griz before I'd interrupted them.

I grabbed my purse off the coffee table then opened the front door and smiled at the delivery woman.

"Hi," I said.

"Hello." The thin woman with thick, dark hair, held three pizza boxes piled on top of each other. "Three fully-loaded pizzas, hold the capers on the one."

"Sacrilege," I said. "I love the capers in the sauce. Gives the dish a real zing."

The woman nodded and swallowed, swaying on the spot.

"Are you all right?" I asked, and took the pizzas from her then placed them on the side table next to one of the armchairs. "You look pale."

"Fine," she said. "I'm fine."

I fished a few bills out of my purse and handed them over. "Do I know you from somewhere?" I asked. "Sorry, you look really familiar."

"Francesca Russo," she said, as she tucked the money away into a pouch around her waist, her fingers trembling and slipping on the zipper.

Francesca? This was Sal's wife. Well, his widow, now. What on earth was she doing out on deliveries?

"Is everything OK?" Griz asked from the sofa.

"Fine," Francesca repeated.

"You look sick," I said. "Why don't you come in and rest for a second? I can get you a glass of water?"

"I have other deliveries to make." She gestured over her shoulder, back down the path. A beat up Honda was parked out front, the worn sign for Sal's Pizzeria painted along its side in reds and greens. "Don't want to be late."

Francesca made to turn, but stumbled and nearly fell. She caught herself on the balustrade next to Grizzy's front step.

"You need medical attention," I said, then looked back at Grizzy. "Can you call the hospital? An ambulance?"

"Right away." Griz grabbed her phone off the coffee table. Arthur rose from the sofa, a frown wrinkling his forehead, and walked over.

"I told you," Francesca croaked. "I'm fine." But she hadn't let go of the railing, and her knuckles were white. Her back had gone stiff. "I just need a moment. I think I ate something that was wrong... just a case of stomach —" she coughed and tipped forward.

Arthur brushed past me and caught her as she collapsed.

I clamped my jaw. *Not another one. Please, let her be all right.*

"What's going on?" Grizzy appeared next to me, her cellphone against her ear.

"She's collapsed," I said. "Arthur, is she—?"

The detective pressed to fingers to her throat, his expression grave. "No," he said. "She's got a pulse. I think she's just passed out. But we should still get her to a hospital."

"The ambulance is on its way," Grizzy said.

It was a relief to hear, but my mind whirred to action anyway. Was it any coincidence that Francesca, Sal's wife, had also taken ill, so shortly after he'd died? What if there was more to this than met the eye? Heavens knew, I didn't want anything to happen to her or anyone else in Sleepy Creek.

The ambulance arrived shortly after, its sirens whooping and lights flashing. Francesca hadn't stirred, and Arthur had kept her still in case there was an internal injury. The medics took her away on a stretcher.

"Oh, Chris," Grizzy said, "I hope she's going to be OK."

"Me too."

The medics surrounded the stretcher, wheeled it to the back of the ambulance, but stopped before placing her in it. One of them said something, just out of earshot, and a flurry of activity broke out. Arthur approached the van and spoke to a medic that wasn't busy. Finally, he came back to the house, opening the gate to let himself in, shaking his head.

"What's wrong?" Grizzy asked. "Is she going to be OK?"

Arthur didn't reply.

I peered past him at the stretcher Francesca lay upon. The medic standing next to it pulled a sheet over her body.

"I need you two to go back inside. I'm calling Detective Balle out here."

And that was it. Another murder in Sleepy Creek, right on our front doorstep.

6

I had never put too much stock in coincidences. What were the chances that lightning would strike twice or three times or even four times in exactly the same spot? Slim to none. I'd have to look it up later to see if I was wrong about that, but, for now, the analogy would have to do.

Three murders in Sleepy Creek since I'd arrived. Four, if I counted Sal and dismissed the cholesterol claims. What did that mean? That something was up in this town, and it wasn't the sky.

I sat next to Grizzy on the sofa in the living room, staring at the images that flashed on the muted TV.

The detectives were outside doing what they did best. Surveying the scene, speaking to a forensic specialist who'd likely had to drive in from Logan's Rest for this, and generally attracting far too much attention.

"Everyone's going to be talking about this tomorrow," Grizzy said, craning her neck to peek out of the living room windows.

The curtains were open, the streetlamps on as usual and casting light over the gathering crowd of Sleepy Creekers. One after the other, they had arrived, whether by car or on foot, and they stood around, shaking their heads and pointing at the front of the house, chattering, gossiping behind their hands.

"Mona's out there," Grizzy groaned.

Mona was the biggest and most vitriolic gossip in the whole town. If she was out there, the story of Francesca's death would have spread like wildfire through the Sleepy Creek within the next hour. And with embellishments too. Likely, I'd be the one who somehow took the blame, or Grizzy even. Mona didn't like either of us.

"Oh boy." I scraped my hand over my forehead.

Detective Balle entered the living room from outside and nodded to us. "I'm going to need to take some statements, and then I'm going to ask you ladies to pack a bag each and leave the house."

"What?" Grizzy and I lurched forward in unison.

"You've got to be kidding me," I said. "She died on the front porch. It wasn't like—"

"I'm sorry, Miss Watson, Miss Lewis, but given the history of murders on this property, we're going to have to close this place off and do a thorough search."

I pinched the bridge of my nose. Why did this kind of thing always happen to us? For heaven's sake, it wasn't like Francesca had been stabbed or shot on our front step. She'd collapsed. Still, I understood that the handsome detective—I had to stop thinking of him like that—needed to do this.

"This is so bad," Grizzy said.

"Where are we going to stay?" I asked. "And don't you dare say what I think you're going to say. Because that's just—"

"Curly can't go to any of the motels. And I don't think the Sleepy Dreams Guesthouse accepts pets."

"Don't you say it, Griselda Lewis."

"We'll have to ask Missi and Vee."

I groaned. Missi and Vee would be kind enough to take us in, of course, but it would mean dealing with Missi's scrutiny, strange comments, and her clear disdain for my lack of energy in the mornings. Lord knew I loved the woman, but there was only so much a girl could take.

"But, but..." I struggled to find an excuse. There was none.

"That settles it then. I'll call them," Grizzy said.

Arthur entered the living room and came over, looking strangely out of place in his plain cloths and neat slicked hair. He cleared his throat twice, in rapid succession, then beckoned to Griselda. "May I speak to you for a moment?"

Griselda walked over to him, and they stepped into the kitchen and out of earshot, leaving me and the hand—no, the detective, alone.

Liam Balle, the man who'd reported me to the Chief back in Boston for my overzealous investigation of the last murder in Sleepy Creek, gave me a look that would curdled milk. It helped diminish how attractive he was.

"Do I need to tell you that you're not supposed to get involved in this, Miss Watson?" Liam asked.

"Hmm, do you think it will matter if you do?" I countered. It was his attitude that got to me. He wasn't usually this hostile, and I didn't understand why he had to be this way now. It wasn't like he'd just witnessed a stranger dying on his front porch.

"Don't do that, Watson. Don't give me your snark and sarcasm now. This is serious."

"I know that," I said, and frowned at him. "Are you...? Liam."

"What?" He had been faffing with his pocket, struggling to draw a notebook and pen out of it.

"Are you OK? You seem tenser than usual." He clicked his ballpoint frenetically. Finally, his demeanor softened. He walked over and took a seat on the sofa. Not close enough that we touched, but certainly close enough that his cologne washed over me.

I tried blocking my nose from the inside against that warm, woodsy scent, but it didn't work. My stomach betrayed me by sprouting several swarms of roving butterflies.

Liam ran his fingers through his thick dark hair, and I swallowed.

What was wrong with me? I couldn't think of anything other than the fact that I hadn't run a brush through my hair since this morning and that my mascara was probably smudged. Curse Detective Balle and his natural animal magnetism.

"I shouldn't tell you," Liam said, at last.

"Has it got to do with work?"

"Yeah." He clicked his ballpoint again. "I've been taking some heat from the captain at the station. He's not happy about what's going on in Sleepy Creek. Apparently, Mayor Samson has been putting pressure on him to keep the town clean for the upcoming Spring Food Fair."

"Clean, huh? Clean of trash or murder?"

"Murder." Balle turned his head and our gazes met. His was sharp and strong, and a caramel brown. "We've never had this many cases in rapid succession. No town is completely free of trouble, but this is... the captain thinks the cases might be connected. But I can't see it."

I happened to agree with the captain, then. But I was biased. My mother had died in

Sleepy Creek years ago, and her case had gone cold. The fact that the death of Loopy Paul, just three weeks ago, had been tenuously linked to her death was yet another lead I had pursued. And l hadn't come up with any real answers.

And what were the chances that all of these murders had happened so close at hand? Right in front of me on all four occasions. It wasn't like I was a trouble magnet. No, I usually caused the trouble through my impulsive investigation. It was what had landed me on sabbatical in the first place.

"You can't see it?" I asked.

"No, not really. Not yet. There are leads, but no connections. For instance, Haley Combes' death and the—" he cut off, and his eyes narrowed, as if he'd only just realized who he was talking to. "Never mind. We're not here to talk about my problems. I need to take your statement and ask you a few questions, Miss Watson."

I was more than happy to cooperate. But

the truth was, already, my mind was aflame with possibilities—aflame, indeed, like a delicious Chicken Burger. Francesca was dead, Detective Balle clearly thought it was a murder or we wouldn't have been having this conversation, and Sal? That remained to be seen.

Liam shot questions my way, and I answered them, nothing the state of his hair—messed, fingers he'd run through it too many times—and the dark circles under his eyes. His skin was paler too, eyes bloodshot. Too much time in front of the PC at his desk?

"And what about Francesca?" he asked. "How well did you know her?"

"Not well at all."

"You're sure about that."

"Yeah, why?"

"Because we found a letter on her person addressed to you. It seemed she was trying to slip it into your pizza box, but didn't manage before she collapsed," Liam said.

"A letter? Where is it? What did it say?"

The detective hesitated.

"It directly involves me, Balle. I deserve to know."

"It was vague. She wanted to meet with you to talk about something. Any idea what it was?"

"None. I didn't know her. Are you sure the letter was addressed to me?"

"Positive."

"I don't know what that's about."

Balle stared at me for a long moment. "That's all I need," he said, at last, and rose from the sofa. "I'll escort you upstairs so you can pack a bag before you leave."

"That's OK." I couldn't get the words out quick enough. The last thing I needed was for him to see the inside of the frilly pink guest room.

"I have to, Christie," he said, softly. "You know that."

"Of course you do." I barely kept the groan at bay. He had to ensure I didn't tamper with any evidence. So here we were again, at the start of another murder investigation in Sleepy Creek, with the prospect of a night at Missi and Virginia's place ahead.

Could things in Sleepy Creek get more complicated? I had the feeling I didn't want the answer to that.

7

The following day was a Saturday, and I had the morning and afternoon off for a change. Spending it at home with a good book would have been my number one choice, if that book hadn't also been a murder mystery and reminded me of exactly what was going on in Sleepy Creek.

Or what wasn't going on. What if the detectives couldn't figure out what had happen?

There was also the fact that I was now relegated to the futon in Missi and Vee's apartment, and that Missi had promised to beat the God into me if I so much as messed a crumb in here. Had to love the woman.

Curly, for what it was worth, had stayed in her kitty carry case overnight, peering out of the opening and refusing to step out until food had been placed directly in front of her.

I paced back and forth in the living room, my hands tucked behind my back, drawn to the window and the street outside. I'd already had my morning coffee, but the smells from the bakery next door were a consistent temptation.

And if I went down there I'd have the chance to chat to Dolores.

Dolores who had put up a huge clapboard sign outside her bakery—***SPECIALS ALL DAY IN CELEBRATION OF THE END OF THE PIZZA-CAKE WAR***. It was both jokey and crass. Disrespectful too, but there was a line out there that moved pretty quickly, and folks who went in, exited minutes later with little bags bearing Dolores' Bakery's logo.

Basically, this was profit for Dolores. Sal's death was profit.

"Gross," I said, under my breath.

"Is this your plan for the foreseeable future?" Missi spoke behind me, her voice whip-crack sharp.

I managed not to jump, thank goodness. If I had, Missi would never have let it slide. I turned my head and gave her my best 'I'm scrutinizing you' face.

Missi rolled her crystal blue eyes. "Oh please, Watson, you know better than to try that with me. Now, is this what you plan on doing with your day? Lying around up here and waiting for something to happen?"

"I'm not lying around," I said, and gestured to the futon. "I'm standing around. There's a difference."

"Hmm."

"Shouldn't you be in the antique shop?" I asked.

The twins owned the Terrible Two's Antiques store downstairs. Missi and Vee were passionate about two things: antiques and burgers. "I'm taking a break," Missi said. "I came to fetch my handbag, not that it's any of your business, Watson."

More like she'd come to harass me. "I was just leaving."

"To go where?"

"Get a bite to eat."

"From where?"

"When did you become the detective?" I asked. "Did we have a Freaky Friday moment without me realizing it?"

Missi harrumphed. "If you're going to the Burger Bar, you can come with us. The sun's out today. Lovely weather."

I raised an eyebrow at her.

"Unless, of course, you're going to the bakery downstairs. They do a wonderful croissant."

"I know."

A silence followed, and Missi pruned up her lips, grabbed her handbag off the side table and slung it over her shoulder. It was huge, big enough to hide a pepper grinder or a bottle of hot sauce, or, potentially, a burger. "Fine," she said, "keep your secrets. Just don't keep them in here."

"Yeah, yeah, yeah." I picked up my spare key off the coffee table, tucked it into the pocket of my jeans, then tied up my hair and followed her out through the main exit. It led directly down into the back of the antique shop.

I wound between old books and furniture, carvings and statuettes, and waved to Vee before stepping out onto the sidewalk outside. It was a perfect day to grab a bite to eat, maybe take a walk in the park, sit by the fountain, catch up with some of the residents. Go shopping even.

There wasn't that much to do in Sleepy Creek, but I grasped at the possibilities to keep myself from taking a left turn and joining the fast-moving queue that disappeared inside Dolores' Bakery.

It didn't work.

I joined the back of the line. My thoughts whirred. Dolores profiting off Sal and Francesca's deaths, mostly Sal's but still. People chattering and gossiping. Francesca had tried to get me to meet with her. Why? What had she wanted to tell me? Was it a co-incidence that she'd died only moments later? I couldn't switch off.

"—don't think she really did it, do you?" a man said, up ahead.

The longstanding belief was that women were huge gossips. I'd figured out, in my time in both Boston and Sleepy Creek, that men talked an equal amount of manure.

The one ahead of me in line held a woman's hand. She was a head shorter than him, and leaned against his side like she couldn't stand without him. "You never know in this town. Anything's possible."

"Anything? Unicorns in tutus and pigs in silk and—"

"Stop." She reached up and pinched his

wobbly double chin. "You know I don't like it when you talk like that."

He went quiet as the row shifted forward, rapidly, and more people exited the bakery with their treats or cups of coffee.

"But what if it's really her?"

"I don't know, honey bunny, but if it is—

"Shush, shush, there she is." The man placed his arm around his partner and drew her close.

The crowd and shifted, and Nelly Boggs, the florist, stepped out from within. Wherever she went, heads turned and eyes narrowed. She blushed a bright pink and hurried down the street, away from the watchers.

They were talking about her.

Nelly, guilty of murder? I would have snorted if the guy in front of me hadn't mentioned pigs in silk.

I slipped out of the line and followed the florist down the street. She crossed it, glancing both ways three times, her head swiveling and her mousy brown hair duller than usual, then entered the florists'. The glass door with its flowery, curling writing slammed closed behind her.

"What's this about?" I followed her across the road then ducked into the shop. I was embraced by the smell of flowers. Flowers so weren't my thing. The only scent I really enjoyed flower-wise was lavender, and even that in moderation.

I stopped, frowning.

Rows and rows of flowers in metal buckets on wooden tables filled the room. There was a counter at the front, but Nelly wasn't behind it.

I took another step into the shop, and my nose itched. I sneezed.

A cry sounded from behind the counter, and Nelly Boggs popped up from the floor. "Oh my goodness," she said, and flattened her hair to her cheeks, tucked it behind her ears. "Christie. Is—? I didn't see you there."

"You OK?" Bit of pastry on her cheek, red eyes, puffy—had been crying. Hair unwashed.

Her long cardigan's sleeves were stained on the ends like she'd been... what, working with dirt? That would've made sense if this was a nursery, not a florist's.

"I'm fine," Nelly squeaked, but her bottom lip trembled.

"Are you?"

"No." A tear escaped her eye and traveled down her cheek.

"What's wrong?"

"It's everything." Nelly scuttled out from behind the counter and moved toward the door. She peered out, grabbed hold of the sign that hung against it and flipped it from OPEN to CLOSED. "Sorry, I just— there's no point."

"No point in what?" I asked.

"Keeping the store open. Everyone who's come in here today has only wanted to talk to me about Sal or Francesca. And not because they want flowers for the funeral, either."

"Then why?"

"They think... they think I did it. That I

killed them both." Nelly burst into tears and lifted her stained sleeves to her face and wiped it. "But I didn't, Christie, I swear. I didn't do anything. I just—"

I came forward and put my arm around her shoulder. I wasn't good at this kind of thing, but sheesh, I had to try. Couldn't just let her cry like this. I patted her awkwardly, and her sniffles slowed.

Nelly sighed. "I miss her."

"Who?"

"Francesca. That's what makes this worse," she continued, "she was a close friend of mine, and now she's gone, and I feel like it's all my fault because everyone else is saying that I was involved when really I wasn't and I just—"

"Take a breath, Nelly," I said. "You're going to pass out."

She took several.

"You and Francesca were close?" I asked, once she'd finished her yoga breaths.

"Yes. Very close. Poor Francesca. She loved Sal so dearly. He was sick for a week before the... incident. She couldn't get him to go to the hospital. Every time she asked him to go, he said that he wouldn't because it was what 'they' wanted."

"They?"

"I have no idea." Nelly shrugged. "And now poor Fran is gone too. She was such a good person. She didn't deserve to go like that. I mean, no one does. And now, everyone—"

I hugged her again as she dissolved into a flurry of tears. "Listen, it's OK. Why don't you come by to Missi and Vee's tonight? We're all having dinner there. You can talk about how you feel and so on and yeah, everyone will be really supportive." More supportive than I could be. If only Griselda was here—she was the emotional one. She'd know the right thing to say to Nelly to calm her down.

"You would do that? Even though everyone thinks—"

"Forget about what everyone thinks," I said, and waved a hand at her. "It only matters what the cops think. Come on over tonight. Missi and Vee won't mind. We can toast to Francesca. She's in a better place now."

Nelly nodded. "You're right. I-I will. Thanks, Christie. I needed to talk to someone about this."

"Listen, you can talk to me anytime." And by that, I meant she could give me leads on who had murdered Sal and Francesca.

Another two murders in Sleepy Creek. And a 'they' who Sal had been afraid of? Or defiant against? A 'they.' Could 'they' be the Somerville Spiders, the very same group I suspected had murdered my mother over twelve years ago?

"Christie?"

"Hmm?"

"Sorry, you were staring at my forehead."

"Oh!" I shook my head. "Listen, I'll see you tonight. Stop by around seven."

"I'll be there."

And so would I, with my list of questions in hand. I struggled to name Nelly as a suspect—she was the 'wouldn't hurt a wasp if it stung her' type—but I had to keep my options open. Anyone could be connected to the murder.

And the murders might be connected to my mom.

"Here we go again," I muttered, as I let myself out onto the street.

8

We sat around the small table in the twins' kitchen, inhaling the delicious smells of Missi's Mac and Cheese.

Nelly had dried her eyes and changed out of her stained cardigan, Grizzy looked worse for wear after a gossip-imbued day in the Burger bar, and Vee was, well, Vee. Neat and elderly and sweet enough to give you a toothache.

"It's almost done," Missi announced, from

her position in front of the oven. "Give it another two minutes to brown the cheese."

Missi had never struck me as the nurturing type, but I'd stood corrected a few times when it came to the twins. Missi was a terrific cook, and Vee had her snappy moments when she didn't get her way.

"Are you all right, dear?" Vee asked, and patted Nelly on the back of her hand. "You look a bit pale."

"I'm fine, thank you." Nelly took another sip of her soda—it was a foreign brand I didn't recognize, but Virginia swore it was the best soda we'd ever taste. Dark and fizzy and way too sweet. "The sugar is helping."

"Good," Missi said. "You need to keep your wits about you in this town. Never know who's waiting to stab you in the back."

Nelly paled.

"Poor choice of words," I noted.

Missi pursed her lips, but didn't argue. She bent to check the crispiness of the cheese instead.

"My sister meant that there are people here who are all about the gossip."

Griz sighed. "She's right. I had about a million people come into the Burger Bar this morning and cross-question me about what I saw and where I was and who'd been the victim. A few of them even wanted to know if I'd done it."

"What?" I glared at her. "Who said that?"

"The usual. Mona. You know how she is. Always willing to stick her nose where it doesn't belong."

"Sounds like someone we know." Missi flicked the back of my ponytail with her dishcloth. "No offense meant."

"What, you're comparing me to Mona? At least I'm doing this for a good cause."

Grizzy turned toward me. "Doing what, exactly?"

"Nothing. I meant—"

"The last time you investigated, you got a warning. You won't be so lucky next time, and you know it." Griz pointed at me.

"I know, I know."

"Wait, what?" Nelly had set her glass down on the table with a clunk. "What do you mean by investigated?"

I glanced first at Grizzy then at Vee. Both women shrugged. It wasn't a secret to them that I was about finding the truth. I'd figured that most of the folks in Sleepy Creek had to know by now. A few of them had even approached me with information of their own accord during my investigation the week before. "I sometimes look into these types of things, Nelly. Unofficially, of course."

"So, you could help me find who did it."

"Now, I wouldn't go as far as to say that." If I wanted to prove anything, I needed evidence, and that was in seriously short supply this time around. All I knew was that people hated Sal, he'd had high cholesterol, and that Fran had been a victim as well. Hmmm, and then there'd been that mention of 'they.'

"Christie, you're doing it again." Griz clicked her fingers in front of my face.

"I know," I said. "I was just... thinking."

"Always a dangerous thing for you to do." Missi opened the oven door, and the scent of cheese and noodles and delicious melty sauce rushed out into the kitchen. She drew the dish out and placed it on the counter, then switched her oven off. "Now it has to rest."

"But..." Nelly fiddled with her soda glass, looking down into its depths, then up at me. "But you could help, couldn't you? You could prove that I didn't do it. That I never would have done anything to hurt Sal and Francesca."

I didn't have an answer for that. Helping Nelly was hugely tempting, so was investigating, but I oscillated between going for it and hesitating again. Because I would get caught. I was bad at breaking the law, even if breaking the law meant trying to keep the integrity by investigating a case surreptitiously.

"She can't help," Grizzy said. "I'm sorry, Nelly, but if she does, she'll get in a lot of trouble."

"Oh." Nelly's shoulders sagged. "All right, I understand."

"Let's not be hasty," I said. "Maybe there's something Nelly can tell us that would lay some light on the whole investigation."

"Oh boy." Grizzy shook her head, her blonde locks swaying in her ponytail. "Here we go."

"Nelly," I said, doing my best to ignore her and the whines of hunger from my stomach. Surely, the Mac and Cheese had rested for long enough, now? "What can you tell me about Francesca and Sal? Did they have any enemies that you know of?"

"Enemies? No, not really. I mean, Sal had plenty of enemies."

"Can say that again," Missi muttered. "The man was a walking insult."

"Don't start," Vee hissed. "He was merely pointing out that you'd stepped in something. He wasn't saying you had put your foot in it."

"I fail to see the difference."

"That's because you're stubborn. Now,

how's that Mac and Cheese coming on?" Vee asked.

"It'll be ready when it's ready."

"But—"

"Don't rush me, sister, it has to be perfect."

"Stubborn as a mule," Virginia sighed.

"Sorry, Nelly, what were you saying about enemies?" I asked.

"Sal had a lot of them." The florist lifted her glasses off her face and polished them, blinking owlishly beneath the kitchen fluorescents. "The most obvious one was Dolores the baker. You know, she really didn't like him. And I don't mean in a professional sense. Every time they ran into each other, they fought."

But hadn't we seen Sal fighting with Nelly too? Interesting. "Anyone else?"

"Not that I can think of. Oh, but I know that Francesca and Sal had some extra stress lately."

"About what?"

"Distant relatives that moved in," Nelly said. "A friend of Franny's family and then Sal's cousin. They were struggling to pay the bills already, and after the others arrived, well, things only got more stressful. At the time, I figured that was why Sal was so ill. Stress."

So, out of town relatives had come to stay, Sal had made plenty of enemies, and now he was dead. That got me no closer to the truth, but it was something. The fact that the family had been having financial troubles was another point of intrigue. Money and love were leading motivations for murder. When it wasn't mob or drug-related, of course.

"All right," Missi said, behind us. "It's ready." She lifted the mac and cheese dish onto the table and set it down, then brought out the plates and the cutlery.

I spooned a massive helping of cheesy oozy goodness onto my plate, tucked in and crunched on something salty and flavorful. "Wow, is that...?"

"Bacon," Missi said, proudly. "My little

stroke of genius. Brings a whole new level to the mac and cheese, don't you think?"

"It's delicious," I replied.

We filled our bellies to the brim, and I could almost feel the pounds packing on. After, we all settled in the living room for some coffee and cookies, and Nelly told us more about Francesca—how lovely she'd been, how caring, and how Nelly had always thought that Francesca deserved better than Sal.

"Of course, that's a horrible thing to say, but it was true. Sal was mean, and she deserved better."

"Was he cruel to her?" Virginia asked, and gave a little shudder to show what she thought of that.

"No, not cruel, I don't think. She didn't complain about stuff like that. Just that he had bad habits and maybe a bit of a wandering eye."

I raised an eyebrow. Money issues, check. Potential love issues, check. If Francesca hadn't passed on herself, she would definitely have been a suspect.

"What do you think, Christie?" Nelly turned to me. "Would you be able to get to the bottom of it? People know that I didn't approve of Sal. That's the only reason why I can think they'd believe I'd had anything to do with it."

Grizzy didn't say anything, but she did throw the slightest head shake in my direction. She didn't want me to put myself in jeopardy—Chief Wilkes had already given me my final warning. The next time I was found out, my job in Boston was gone.

Will that be so bad?

Of course, it would be bad. It would be losing everything I'd worked for. The only reason I'd become a detective in the first place was to take after my mother, and, hopefully, when I was in the right frame of mind, to investigate what had actually happened to her.

I couldn't do any of that if I wasn't a detective.

"Please?" Nelly asked.

I dragged my tongue over my bottom lip. "I'll see what I can do," I said, at last.

"Oh, thank you, Christie, you're a life saver." She leaned back in her chair and exhaled. "I don't know how I'll manage if everyone thinks I did it."

That statement piqued my interest. Why did Nelly care so much? Why was she worried if the cops would ultimately prove her innocent by arresting the real culprit?

My suspect list had already formed, and I went down it mentally as I sipped on my coffee and chewed on Virginia's freshly baked oatmeal raisin cookies. First up was Dolores, but not far down that line was Nelly herself.

One could never be too careful in Sleepy Creek.

9

Dolores' Bakery was open every day of the week. It was great for me, since I loved her croissants with chocolate dipping sauce, and for Griz, who desperately needed some time off from the Burger Bar, as well.

The specials were still on, the clapboard's writing bright and attractive in red chalk, but the bakery was relatively quiet this early on a Sunday morning. Most folks were on their way into church, or getting ready to go, and the early comers to the bakery were all dressed in their Sunday best.

"I'm starving," Grizzy said, as we joined the short line.

The place smelled divine, a combination of baking cookies and fresh roasted coffee beans. The inside was cheery, as well, with large open windows that let in light onto the boarded floors, tables with quaint white tablecloths and rickety mismatched chairs.

Menus spanned the walls in curly writing, items and prices listed next to each other in gold font.

"Everything looks so good," Griz said.

I nodded.

"What?"

"Nothing, why?"

"No, no, Christie, you can't fool me. You know, I wasn't born yesterday." Griz pursed her lips.

"I can vouch for that. I was there yesterday. No baby would be allowed to eat that much Mac 'n Cheese in one sitting."

"You're too much," Griz replied. "And you know what I'm talking about. I don't suppose it's a coincidence we just so happen to have come here for our morning snack?"

"I would have gone to the Burger Bar, but there's only so many burgers a person can eat."

"Speak for yourself."

"Yet more proof that you were not, indeed, born yesterday." I couldn't avoid her questions for long, though. "And yeah, OK, I'm not just here for the delicious croissants and the fattening chocolate dip. She asked me to help her, Griz, so I'm going to help her."

"I'd say you were a kind soul, but I know helping Nelly isn't your only priority. You've got the bug again." Griz poked me in the side.

"Ow. That wasn't fair."

"Neither is putting yourself at risk like this. Though, it's hypocritical of me to say it. When my cousin was in trouble, I helped you investigate."

"And you can help me now," I said.

"How?"

"By ordering my croissant while I go speak to that woman in the corner. The one crying softly into her apron."

"Oh dear."

The more I looked around the place, the stranger the inside of the bakery seemed. Firstly, it was far too empty, and secondly... the folks who wore the aprons or stood behind the counters all-seemed tight-lipped, apart from the one waitress who was tear-streaked instead.

"Be right back," I said.

"Try not to make it worse," Griz whispered.

I walked to the table in the corner, right near the front counter, and stopped in front of the waitress. She wore a Dolores' Bakery apron, the woman's name splashed across her chest, and held the end of it to her face, dabbing furiously beneath her eyes. Her name tag read: Jessa-May.

"Hello." I reached into my handbag. I brought out a pack of Kleenex and offered it to her. Rule number two on my mother's go-to life hacks list had been: always carry a pack of Kleenex in your purse, you never know when you'll need a tissue, whether it's for tears or to remove an item from the scene of a crime without contaminating the evidence.

"Hello." Jessa-May's green eyes were bloodshot. "Do you need help? I'm sorry, I'm on my break, I—"

"Here." I waggled the pack of Kleenex at her. "Take one. You look like you need it."

"Thank you," she said, and took the entire pack. I let it slide. "Sorry, I can't help anyone, right now."

I sat down across from her and placed my forearms on the table, the fabric dragging on my thin-knit sweater. "That's all right. I don't need any help. I saw you were feeling a bit... um, down, and I thought I would ask if you're OK?"

Jessa-May's bottom lip trembled. "No, not really. I'm not OK at all. That mean woman." She held herself completely still as she spoke, her mouth making shapes, her nostrils flaring. "She's not even a woman, she's a creature."

"Who?" I asked.

"Dolores." The way she said it, I half-expected a murder of crows to appear and smash into the front window.

"The owner of the bakery?"

"Yes," Jessa-May hissed. "She's a horrible… I can't even put it into words." Jessa was young, probably in her early twenties, her blonde hair tied up in a messy bun atop her head. Strands stuck up from it, and trembled as she spoke, as if she was shaking from the sheer ferocity of the words leaving her.

"What happened?" I asked, my gaze dancing away toward the counter. What if Dolores appeared now? Would she take issue with me talking to one of her employees?

"She yelled at me," Jessa said. "Told me I was useless. She came down from upstairs in an absolute rage and took it out on me because I was the only one within range." Jessa sniffed. "That's what I get for arriving on time, not like the others. They were all late, and I—"

"Where is she now?" I asked.

"Stormed off. Apparently, she's got an appointment today." Jessa-May's tears had dried, but the end of her nose was a little red. "And I bet I know who it's with."

"Who?"

Griz was at the front of the queue ordering for us both.

"The cops," Jessa said, shifting to sling one arm over the back of her chair. "That delicious detective, Liam Balle? She's going to see him."

My chest squeezed, and my eyebrows drew inward. *Delicious? Really? Isn't he a little too old for you, Jessa?* I buried my jealousy—I wasn't actually jealous, there had to be another reason for this—and leaned in. "To the cops? What for? Has it got something to do with what happened to Sal?"

"And Francesca," Jessa-May whispered. "I hate to say it, but I'd believe it if she'd murdered them both. I know what kind of a woman Dolores really is. She's mean, and she thinks too much of herself. And the once, I saw her right outside of Sal's pizzeria after it was closed. In the middle of the night."

Jessa was so angry, there was barely any need to press her for information. She freely offered it up.

"What do you mean? How?"

"Oh, it was about a week ago," Jessa said, scooching forward so that she leaned right over the table. She sniffed and dabbed under nose, but kept intense eye contact with me. "I had just gotten back from my mother's place in Logan's Rest. Late bus in. Didn't want to leave too early. And I was hungry, so I thought I'd check if anything was open. You know, sometimes Sal would stay open overnight, just as a big... well, I won't curse, but it was to get back at Dolores for dominating the early morning traffic in Sleepy Creek."

I took mental notes rapidly. Jessa had a splotch of something on her collar, something red. Lipstick? Make up? Ketchup? It wasn't of any consequence, but my eyes kept wandering over to it. Marinara sauce?

"Anyway, I was walking down the street when I saw her, standing there. Pizzeria was closed, but she had her face pressed up against the glass and her hands cupped around it so she could see inside better."

"Jessa!" Another of the waiters called from the counter. "Can you stop crying for five seconds and come help us?"

Jessa-May rolled her eyes and waved a hand over her shoulder. "And that's not all, I saw."

"Yeah?"

"The other day, when I was closing up after the evening diners had left?"

"Yeah?"

"Dolores came in with a package from the hardware store. She ignored me and took it right upstairs, but she dropped the receipt accidentally, and I picked it up." Jessa pressed her lips together, pouting them outward. "She bought poison. Rat poison. This place doesn't have any rats. Dolores would never let that happen, so why would she buy rat poison, hmm? What's that about?"

I kept my expression impassive. "What did you do with the receipt?"

"Huh?" Jessa frowned. "Oh, nothing. I threw it away. I didn't think it mattered at the time, but you can bet that if that sexy guy detective comes back round here, I'll be telling him all about this. And then he can lock her up and throw away the key, because I just know it was her. I just know it."

"Jessa! She's on her way back!" one of the other waiters yelled.

Jessa-May jumped up like she'd been electrocuted and rushed away without another word, taking my pack of Kleenex with her. Now, what would I do if I ran into irrefutable evidence that needed collecting?

"What was that about?" Grizzy came over, carrying two takeaway cups of coffee and two boxes stacked on top of each other with 'Dolores' Bakery' stamped on each.

"Let's walk to church," I said. "I'll tell you on the way." And it would give me time to work things through.

Dolores buying rat poison. Dolores at the pizzeria. Could it be that simple?

❧ 10 ❧

The Burger Bar bustled on a Sunday afternoon. It always did after church, where people would come in for a burger and a gossip, mostly about Pastor Frank's sermon or whether people really believed his wife had left him simply because he was too committed to his work. The gossip circle was convinced that Mrs. Pastor Frank had skipped town to marry a Pilates instructor.

"It's shameful," Virginia said, dolefully, as the four of us tucked into our burgers.

Martin had opted to run the Sunday shifts in the Burger Bar, and our new waitress, Hedy, was shadowing him around the Burger Bar, practicing for tomorrow when she'd start full-time. The Burger Bar's popularity had grown as spring warmed and the Food Fair grew closer.

Personally, I believed it had something to do with the murders. The restaurant was the hotspot for news.

"—listening to you, at all."

I turned my head, catching the last of Missi's sentence. "Huh?"

"The correct term is 'pardon me,' Watson. Not 'huh?' You wouldn't know the meaning of ladylike if it hit you in the face," Missi sniffed.

"Ladylike? Firstly, that's not my prime inspiration in life. I'd prefer to be respected as a person and an investigator. And secondly, would 'ladylike' really hit me in the face? You see the paradox there, right?"

Missi opened her mouth to argue, but Virginia waved a hand at her. "It's fine, sister," she said, "I don't mind repeating myself. It only means I'll get to order another vanilla shake."

I took the mention of the shake as a segue to slurp on my own.

"I was saying that it's shameful, people gossiping about Pastor Frank like this."

"Shameful," Grizzy echoed, and lifted her cherry off her blob of cream. She gobbled it down. "Do people have nothing better to do?"

"No, I mean, it's shameful that they think his love life—"

"Or lack thereof," Missi interrupted.

"—is important when there's a murderer on the loose. A double murderer." Virginia plumbed the depths of her milkshake with her thick paper straw. "What is that called? Just a double homicide? At what point can we call it a serial killer?"

"Don't say that, Vee," Grizzy whispered. "Someone will hear you. It will spook the customers."

"Darling, you could stand on the table and scream serial killer at the top of your lungs

and it would probably bring in more customers," Missi said, patting Griz on the arm.
"It's the nature of the Sleepy Creek beast."

"It gives me goosebumps," Grizzy said.

"It's not official as to whether the two
deaths are connected," I said, "so I can't say."

"But you want to say, don't you, dear?" Virginia asked, scooching in closer. "Rumor has
it, you were at the bakery this morning."

"Rumor has it?" I asked.

"Fine, I told her," Grizzy put in, between
slurps of strawberry milkshake. "She's got that
way about her, Chris, she gets the information
right out of me."

"Interesting," Vee said, "very interesting.
So Dolores is a suspect?"

"Keep your voice down, please, ladies," I
said. "You know the walls have ears in here."

The front door swung open barely seconds
after the words had left my mouth, and Mona
Jonah and her gossip circle entered the Burger
Bar. They reminded me of a much older ver-
sion of that movie, Mean Girls—they wore

matching leopard-sprint scarves and red lipstick, with horn-rimmed sunglasses to boot.

No, not Mean Girls, they were like the Pink Ladies from Grease. Except with less pink and a whole lot more hairspray.

The chatter in the diner silenced momentarily as people turned and eyed the newcomers. Finally, it resumed again, a few of the older women in the crowd bowing their heads low or avoiding eye contact with the circle.

Mona Jonah whipped her sunglasses off her face, and the other women followed her example. Their beady gazes roved over the place, until, finally, they selected a table right next to ours and made a beeline for it.

Mona clicked her fingers at the new waitress, Hedy, who almost dropped her tray in an effort to rush after her.

"Uh oh," I said, "no way is Hedy going to be able to handle this by herself." The poor girl was just about to graduate from Sleepy Creek High, looking for a job for the approaching summer, slight and with auburn hair that hung in a bob around her face. Her green eyes were doe-like. Easy to mistake as weak.

I made to get up, but Grizzy had already raised her hand for Martin, who rushed over and nudged Hedy toward another table. He smiled at Mona and her circle. "Good morning, ladies."

"It's almost afternoon," Mona sniffed. "We'll take five chicken burgers and five chocolate shakes."

"They even eat the same thing," Grizzy whispered.

"I suspect their digestive systems are synced up." Missi sat back, her eyes sharp at the presence of the women. She definitely didn't like the circle. And the circle definitely didn't like her right back. "You know, they all go number one at the same time."

"Mississippi, we're at the table," Vee hissed, scandalized.

"What? It's not like I said number two."

Virginia opened and shut her mouth,

shock overcoming her, and giving opportunity for me to listen in on the conversation at the circle's booth.

Mona had to have noticed us, but she didn't seem to care much that we were seated right behind her. Maybe, it was because she was with her group and wanted to assert dominance. I could never tell with her.

"Now, where were we?" Mona said, after the orders were taken and the waiter had disappeared. "The case of Sal's death, correct?"

"Yes, Mona." I couldn't see which woman had answered, but she sounded as if she was in a classroom rather than chilling out in a restaurant for a Sunday burger brunch.

"I heard," Mona said, without much need for prompting, "that there's been big trouble in the family. That new cousin of his, Mario? He's apparently been in charge of the pizzeria ever since Sal passed on. Some would say that's very suspicious."

"Would we say that?" one of the women asked.

"Of course, Rebecca. Keep up, for heaven's sake." Mona gave a long-suffering sigh. Ah, the perils of being followed around by a group of lackeys who lived off your every word. I had little to no sympathy for the woman. She was a plague.

"Apparently, he's the one who's hosting a dual ceremony for Sal and Francesca. On a Tuesday. Who in their right mind has a memorial service on a Tuesday? Don't answer that, Rebecca, it was a rhetorical question."

I met Missi's gaze across the table. Her lips had thinned, this time to withhold the laughter that had her shoulders shaking.

"And he's inviting everyone in Sleepy Creek to attend. Everyone. Even Dolores. Now, if that's not suspicious, I don't know what is." Mona tapped her fingers on the tabletop with a clickety-click. "Clear your schedules, girls, we'll be there on Tuesday. We're going to find out just what this Mario Russo guy is hiding."

"What if he's not hiding anything?"

"Don't be ridiculous, Kimberly-Ann. Everyone has something to hide."

The words rang in my ears, not only because Mona had a particularly sonorous voice, but because they were true. Everyone did have something to hide.

And this memorial service sounded like the perfect place to start snooping around for the truth.

So much for keeping your nose clean.

❧ 11 ❧

Everyone who was anyone in Sleepy Creek had been invited to attend the memorial service for Sal and Francesca. And that meant all the town's residents had turned up. Sal and Francesca had lived in the suburbs with a relatively large house and back yard. Plenty of space for people to gather, to talk, and to eat after the church service.

Tables had been set out, and a few fold-out chairs, as well as an entire spread of food—

tables were laden with treats that the family had supplied and that the Sleepy Creekers had brought themselves, to help the Russo's in their time of mourning.

"This has to be the worst apple pie I've ever tasted," Missi said, beside me.

"Aren't you delightful?"

"Watson, it's one thing to host a memorial service that's more of a party—" she nodded toward the live band now setting up at the other end of the garden, right between two oversized pictures of Sal and Francesca, "—it's another entirely to force substandard food on one's guests. It isn't done."

I opened my mouth to argue but gave it up. Missi wouldn't change her opinion, and I was far more interested in the hosts of the memorial after-party than I was the dry apple pie. Stale pastry too.

A whooping cry rang out and applause followed, as a slim, tan man approached the band and lifted a microphone from a stand on the wooden platform at the back of the garden. He smiled around at the gathering of people, shot off a few finger guns like he'd just won the lottery, then cleared his throat.

The mic squealed.

Missi grunted.

I inserted a finger into my ear and wiggled it around.

"What's going on?" Grizzy stepped up beside me, carrying a piece of pizza on an oil-soaked paper plate.

"That's the cousin," Vee whispered, and appeared on Missi's other side. "The one who's taken over the pizzeria and supplied the food for today. Have you tasted the apple pie, sister? Terrible, isn't it?"

"Mortifying." Missi gestured to the half-eaten item on her plate.

"Is this thing on?" The cousin—not balding, but a strong nose, intelligent dark eyes—tapped on the microphone with a gloved hand. Tan leather gloves? On a warm spring day? His clothing was immaculate, I couldn't help noting that. Not a speck of dirt on the powder blue coat sleeves of his suit. *Powder blue at his cousin's memorial service?*

Most of the folks in attendance had opted for the traditional black.

"Heyoooo," the cousin said, and did another finger gun. "How are y'all doing?"

He had an accent that smacked of Boston. It reminded me of 'home' and of my mother, and the Somerville Spiders. Not that I needed reminding.

"I said, how are y'all doing?"

A few of the guests muttered indistinctly. No one was in the mood to cheer or clap. It was a memorial service for heaven's sake.

"Good, good," the cousin continued. "Now, most of you don't know me, so I thought I'd introduce myself before we continue with the festivities. Name's Mario." He spread one arm wide. "First of all, welcome to the Russo household. You're most welcome to use the bathrooms, to sit and chat and enjoy the food. Now, you're all here for ol' Sal and his hot young thing of a wife, Francesca."

"Highly inappropriate," Missi said, loudly.

A few other people nodded.

Mario wasn't fazed. "Sal was my cousin and a good man, for the most part."

Mutters started up in the ground, the grumbling from people who Sal had insulted. Once again, just about everyone in Sleepy Creek.

"And I know he would've wanted everyone to celebrate rather than mourn his passing, so, enjoy the food, enjoy the day, and remember Sal," Mario said. "To Sal and Fran." He lifted his hand, though he didn't have a glass in it, and stared around expectantly.

"To Sal and Frank," the people in the crowd said.

"Great. Now, I've got a special treat from you. I managed to get one of Sal's favorite bands to come out. Please welcome, the Heavy Hitters!" He clapped his free hand against the microphone's side and the noise *thwopped* loudly through the speakers either side of the platform.

Finally, Mario placed the microphone back on its stand and descended from the platform. The band took their positions and struck up a melody that was pure noise.

"Oh my goodness," Virginia said, and lifted her hands to her ears.

"He can't be serious." Missi's face had fallen.

I ignored the ladies and kept my eye on Mario. His attitude intrigued me. Granted, not all cousins were close, but it seemed strange, that he was downright jaunty about his cousin's passing. He bobbed through the crowd, his gait decidedly 'hoppy' and made his way toward the back of the house.

If I could get some time with him alone, perhaps, I might be able to squeeze a little information out. I stepped between the folks who had left the grassy patch in front of the stage—a pilgrimage had started toward the food tables and away from the speakers.

I tailed the suspect through the crowd. He reached the back steps of the house, mounted them, then paused to talk to a woman—long dark hair, glossy around her shoulders, and wearing a fitted black cocktail dress. Tall for a woman. She'd chosen red lipstick and dark eyeshadow. Beautiful, but her gaze was anything but.

She glared up at Mario and spoke fast.

Mario's smile went cold at the eyes. He said something, and I would've given anything to read lips. I swerved through the crowd, walked along the side of the house, pretending to admire the flowerbeds, which were both dry and unkempt, and listened hard.

"—about it here," Mario said. "Don't you have any respect?"

"Then let's go inside."

"Bella, now isn't the time."

"We need to talk about it. Now."

"Fine. Inside. Quickly." They beat a hasty retreat up the back steps and disappeared through the kitchen door, the screen slamming behind them.

I followed them, paused and peered into the dingy kitchen and found it empty. I slipped inside.

Voices traveled from the hall adjacent, loud enough to make out, and I didn't bother trying to get any closer. At least, if someone found me in here, I could say I was on my way to the bathroom or looking for a glass of water.

I affected a casual pose next to the refrigerator—a happy family picture of Fran and Sal caught underneath a pizza slice magnet threatened to fall, and I fixed it in place. I checked my nails.

"—believe you." Mario's voice, gruff and not nearly as obliging as it had been outside.

"This is ridiculous. This is... you can't ignore me Mario. I deserve to be treated with respect too," Bella said, in a voice like treacle.

"Do you?" Mario asked. "You're not even related to this family. You're nothing. I should kick you to the curb, but, hey, can't do that now, can I? What if the cops come back looking for you? Think I'll take the fall? You're wrong about that."

"I didn't do it."

"Yeah, bet that's what they all say."

"Who?"

"You know who," Mario said. "I know you're up to something, and it won't take me long to figure out what it is. Think you're going to get away with it for long?"

"I haven't—"

"I'm done with this conversation. Only reason you're still living here with me is because I'm letting you stay. Got it?"

"It's not your house," Bella snapped. "It was Franny's—"

"If you think that's going to stop me, you're wrong. You know what kind of backup I have, woman."

"You're impossible! You can't expect me to be a part of this," Bella said.

"Get outta here, then. Leave. See how far

that gets you." His voice lowered, and I pushed off from the wall, drew a little closer to the doorway. "I'm warning you, get in my way, and you'll find out exactly what Mario Russo is made out of. Everyone in this town will find out what you've done. Cops included."

"I didn't do anything," Bella replied, again.

"Sure, honey, and I'm Santa Claus."

"There's no talking to you. You won't see sense."

"Then get lost," Mario replied, gruffly.

A door slammed and footsteps approached the kitchen.

My heart skipped a beat, but I kept my attitude cool and sauntered toward the sink. I turned on the faucet. A shape blurred in my peripheral vision—Bella rushing through the kitchen. The screen door slammed behind her, and I switched off the water again.

The conversation swirled through my thoughts. Had Mario just accused Bella of murdering Sal and Francesca? I tried making sense of it, but another set of footsteps, heavier this time, disturbed my thoughts.

"What are you doing in here?" Mario stood next to the kitchen table, his arms folded.

$$\maltese \quad 12 \quad \maltese$$

"Just splashing some water on my face," I said, and gestured to the sink. "Didn't want to walk all the way through to the bathroom, and I wasn't sure where it was."

"Just down the hall."

"Sorry." I flashed a smile and made to walk past him. It would give me the opportunity to take a look at the rest of the house, maybe spy hard evidence, if there was any. Likely, Detective's Cotton and Balle had already gotten their hands on it by now.

"Don't be sorry, be careful."

"I'm usually both," I said. "The band out there drove the sense out of my head."

Mario frowned and shifted on the spot. Good heavens, I'd made it worse somehow. He looked like a Shar Pei puppy. "You don't like the band?" he asked, and pressed a hand to his chest. It was small for a man of his size.

"I'm not into..." I searched for the right word for the music, but I couldn't find anything other than 'garbage' or 'trash.' Cacophony, maybe? It was a combination of electric guitar, cymbal crashes and inarticulate screeching.

Now, I'd been subjected to my fair share of heavy metal, there were all types of music tastes back in Boston and even in the Department, but this wasn't even *good* rock music.

"The Heavy Hitters were Sal's favorite band," Mario said. "We grew up listening to them. They're local."

"You're originally from Sleepy Creek?" I asked.

"Boston born and raised, but I used to come down to visit Sal after he moved here."

"Oh yeah?" I leaned my hands back against the counter, affecting a casual stance. "You guys hung out often?"

Mario shrugged. "As often as cousins do," he said. "Nah, that's not true. Sal and I were pretty close. It's the reason he left me the pizzeria in his will. He trusted me to do the right thing. It's our family's way."

"That makes sense. I'm very sorry for your loss. Sal was..." Another troublesome word search. 'Full of it.' 'Mean.' "He was something else," I finished, hoping it would suffice.

"He sure was. Good as they come."

An awkward silence started up, and I took it as my cue. I doubted I'd get much more out of him without being obvious. No doubt, Mario was worried I'd overheard his conversation with Bella.

He was on my suspect list, and if he realized I was interested, my investigation would be over before it began. *Your investigation. Oh man, you're already in too deep.*

"I'd better get back to the party," I said, and withheld a grimace at calling it that.

"Wait," Mario said. "Wait a second, you didn't even tell me your name." He came over, swaying his arms and puffing his chest out. "You know who I am, of course."

"Mario."

He grabbed my hand, lifted it and brushed his gloved fingers over its back.

Another grimace threatened. I barely kept it at bay.

"And you, lovely lady? What's your name?"

I tugged my hand back, but he clamped down tighter, bent over and pressed his thick lips against my skin. "Your name must be as beautiful as you are."

Cringe.

The screen door opened, and the distraction was enough for me rip out of Mario's grubby paws. The relief didn't last long—Liam stood in the doorway.

He wore a plain, black, button down shirt and had matched it with a pair of worn-in jeans. His dark hair was swept to one side. "Watson," he said, then looked over at Mario, who still had his hand out. "Good afternoon, Mr. Russo."

"Detective Balle." Mario had gone tense. He dropped his arm and took a step away from me.

It was a relief, but only because I'd been on the brink of incapacitating Mario as payback for getting spit on the back of my hand. Naturally, me whipping his arm behind his back and pinning him to the floor wouldn't have gone down well with the detective.

I was already on thin ice.

"Am I interrupting something?" Balle's cheeks were strangely flush, and he stared at me more than he did at Mario.

"Ew, no," I said, before I could stop myself. "I mean, no, detective. I came into the house to freshen up. It's getting a little ... intense outside. I was heading to the bathroom." I nodded toward the archway that led into the rest of the house. "If you'll excuse me."

Liam didn't say anything, but his gaze could've burned a hole through my head and right into the wall behind me.

"Of course," Mario said, breaking the tension. He shuffled a card out of his top pocket, along with a pen, and scribbled on the back of the white square. He handed it to me. "Here, take this. It's my card. My personal cell number is one the back. If you need anything at all, you give me a call."

I took the card, but only because it might wind up being valuable evidence later on. Balle watched the exchanged, his eyes narrowing.

I searched for words to excuse myself, found none, and shrugged instead—always the lady, as Missi would have pointed out. I hurried out of the kitchen and into the hallway, exhaling my relief in a long thin stream of air.

That had been close. Too close. I didn't doubt that Liam's strange attitude in the kitchen had everything to do with me being in close proximity to one of his suspects. What were the chances he would have caught me right at that moment? What if he decided to call Chief Wilkes because I'd interfered again?

I strode down the hall, slowing my pace now I was out of range of the detective and the roving Bostonian with the wettest lips in the state, and peered through open doorways. The bathroom was the first door on the right, but I didn't enter it. Instead, I paused, listening hard.

No sounds of pursuit. No detective sneaking around the corner to catch me snooping.

The first few doors yielded nothing but a living room and dining room and a bedroom that looked as if a tornado had hit it. It felt wrong to snoop in someone's private space, so I moved on.

"Jackpot," I muttered, standing in the doorway to the study.

It was painfully neat in comparison to the rest of the house, with a desk that bore only a laptop, shut, and an in-tray with neatly stacked papers. I leaned back, peered down the hall, then took a breath and entered the room.

I hurried to the desk and popped the lid on the laptop. The hairs on the back of my neck stood on end. It was one thing to investigate a case, but to do this? It sat wrong with me. I was a detective. I usually did this type of search with a warrant and the force of the law at my back.

Hurry. The laptop's login screen appeared. No password. I opened it and started my search. The desktop was empty of icons except for a few folders that pertained to Sal's Pizzeria. I opened them. Nothing. Just books, and I was the furthest from an accountant as it was possible to be.

Emails next—Sal's inbox was full. Looked like Mario hadn't exactly been keeping a handle on his affairs over the past few days. Hmmm.

My gaze fell to an email that was from... Francesca?

"What on earth?"

The subject line read: *Have you signed it yet?*

Why would his wife have emailed him instead of talking to him directly? I clicked open and read the contents.

Sal,

I'm tired of waiting now. I know that this has been a tough time for both of us, but you have to do the right thing.

I can't stand having this in my house for a moment longer. I can't trust you anymore. Please sign the divorce papers.

Fran.

My eyebrows rose. Divorce papers? This *was* unexpected. Sal hadn't exactly been the most popular person around, but a divorce? And the email had been sent days before Sal's death.

The plot thickened. If Francesca had somehow been responsible, or had perhaps worked with someone to murder Sal, then later fallen prey to the very person she'd asked for help ... but, no, that was too much of a stretch without evidence.

I closed the email tab, shut the laptop down then continued my search in the home office. If I could find those papers, I'd know if they'd been signed or not. I opened the desk drawers, but they were empty except for the odd pen or notepad or ball of rubber bands.

The place was uncommonly tidy. Had it been neatened up recently? And if so... why?

Footsteps sounded in the hallway, and I slid the desk drawer shut then ducked down, holding my breath.

Please, don't be Liam. Please, don't be Liam.

The steps tracked down the corridor. Closer, closer, and closer to the study. If they stepped inside and came around the desk, the jig was officially up.

Whoever it was stomped past the opening to the study and continued onward. A door slammed a few minutes later and silence follow.

I let out a breath, got up and hurried from the study, checking the corridor both ways before exiting and creeping through the house. The plangent strumming from the band outside hadn't stopped yet, and the memorial service was far from over, but my investigating was done for the afternoon.

Two dead bodies, the victims had been on the cusp of a divorce, a cousin who seemed too happy to host a memorial service, and a long-lost friend who may or may not have done something... bad.

If I'd thought the previous murder investigations had been complicated, boy, had I been wrong.

This one took the cake. No, the burger. And I was definitely going to find out what flavor it was.

13

"Excuse me, Miss?"

I stood near the back of the Burger Bar, my tray tucked under my arm, my fist pressed to the bottom of my chin, and my behind perched on one of the cushy, red vinyl topped barstools. That memorial service yesterday had been something.

Divorce papers.

And Mario the creep had been convinced that Bella had done it. But done what? Was I even sure it was the murder he'd been referring to? If only I could have asked him out-right. Pfft, that was never going to happen.

"Miss? Hello?"

I'd already put myself in far too much danger by snooping on that laptop. I highly doubted Liam and his partner, Arthur, would fingerprint the laptop, if they hadn't done so already, but the potential made me antsy. I should've brought a pair of latex gloves with me to the service.

Because that wouldn't have been suspicious at all. Me whipping out my gloves and snapping them on before I excused myself to go to the bathroom.

"Hey!"

I jerked upright and dropped my tray. I caught sight of one of the customers, standing next to his table in the center of the restaurant.

"Shoot, sorry," I called out, and got off the stool. I'd told Grizzy I wasn't good at the whole waitressing deal, but I'd definitely un-dersold how bad I was. I hurried over to the customer, putting up a smile that definitely didn't look right on my face.

"I've been calling you for five minutes," the man said, and lowered himself back into his chair. He gestured to his empty milkshake glass. "I wanted to order?"

"I'm so sorry, sir. What can I get for you?"

"I'd like a chicken burger, please," he said. "You got any sauces to go with that? Something like a cheese sauce?"

I rattled off our list of sauces.

"Gimme the spicy relish," the customer said. "And another of these choc shakes."

"Coming right up, sir." I lifted his empty glass off the table. "And sorry about that, again."

He flicked his newspaper open by way of dismissal.

I carried the glass into the kitchen then gave Jarvis the order. Griz was out this morning—she'd decided to take Curly to the vet for a checkup—and I was in charge of the slow time between brunch and lunch. It was meant to be easy, and the restaurant was relatively quiet, but it was near impossible to concentrate on anything but Sal.

It didn't help that the locals who came through kept talking about it, even asking me questions as I served them food.

Ten minutes later, I served the significantly less grumpy customer his burger, fries, relish and shake, then seated myself at the counter again, with my back to it so I could keep an eye on my tables. There were only three of them, currently, though I expected Missi or Vee to come in soon.

I checked my watch, sighing.

My shift ended later this afternoon, and I'd already allocated the time for research on Mario, Bella, and the Russo clan in general. It was odd to me that Sal had been from New York and Mario from Boston.

Somerville Spiders.

Heavens, I had to stop thinking about that. And obsessing over the fact that this case might be related to my mother's.

The bell over the door tinkled, and Nelly from the florist's crashed into the restaurant's interior. She wore a pair of reading glasses, skew on her face, and her hair stuck up on one side. Hadn't had the chance to tie it up, properly? Left the house in a rush.

Why?

"Nelly." I waved her over.

She gasped and practically ran at me. The customers in the restaurant looked up from their tables.

"Whoa, slow down." I put my hands on her shoulders. "What's going on?"

She slumped against me, fat tears welling beneath her glasses. She removed them and wiped her cheeks with the loose sleeves of her sweater. "Sorry," she said. "I didn't know where else to go. It's not like I can talk to F-Fran anymore." The words made it out past the tears, but barely.

"Here, come on. Sit down." I guided her to one of the barstools.

She didn't have a handbag or anything with her.

I checked my tables one last time, found them eating or drinking or reading the newspaper, then circled around to the back of the bar.

"I didn't know who else to turn to."

"I hear they have a confessional booth at The Mother Mary Church?" I flashed a grin at her. It fell flat.

Another tear escaped.

"Sorry," I said, "I'm not good at the emotional stuff. Grizzy's the one who's good at that kind of thing." I searched around for a method of helping her. "Oh! Can I interest you in a milkshake? They always cheer me up."

"Yes, please," she said.

I didn't have my trusty Kleenex in my handbag, thanks to the last woman who'd burst into tears in my vicinity. What was it with everyone and crying this week? I grabbed a pile of napkins from the dispenser and handed them to Nelly then set about preparing a vanilla milkshake.

Nelly dabbed at her cheeks, swallowing every other second.

"You want to tell me about what happened?" I asked, as I brought out the ice cream.

"The police have just pulled me in for questioning. They came right into the florist's. They made me close up shop and everything."

I nearly dropped the tub of ice cream. "What?"

"Yeah. I had to stop halfway through changing the water for the roses," she said.

"Wait, Nelly, they questioned you?"

"Yes, and they took my spit."

"Pardon me?" I coughed. "Your spit?"

"Yeah, you know. They took one of those cotton bud things and put it in my mouth and they collected—"

"Oh, a swab. They swabbed your cheek for DNA?" I asked.

"Yeah."

I shouldn't have been shocked. Nelly was a suspect. Just about everyone in Sleepy Creek who hadn't liked Sal was on the list at this point, but the detectives knew more than I did. What did it mean if they had a warrant for Nelly's DNA? Surely, that they believed she was higher on the list than the other suspects?

Why?

What had she done? What else linked her to the crimes?

I stared at her, blankly, and she stared right back. "I didn't do it," she sniveled. "I can see you're thinking that I did it, but I didn't. And now, everyone else is going to—"

"It's OK," I said, and continued making the shake. "Please, don't cry." I couldn't stand it when people cried. It made my chest feel weird. Like an elephant had decided it was a good place to chill out.

"I don't know what to do. I told them everything I know, but I don't think they believe that I'm telling the truth. They think I did something to Franny. That I poisoned her."

"Why on earth would they think that?" I asked.

"Because they found my fingerprints on the pizza boxes in her home," Nelly said. "The same pizza that she ate just before she died."

I kept my expression blank, but my stomach did a little hop, skip and a leap.

Another clue! So both Francesca and Sal had died after eating pizza from Sal's own restaurant.

"And how did that happen?" I asked.

Nelly hiccuped and pressed her napkin to the end of her nose. "I didn't do it, I swear."

"Nelly, please, calm down. I'm not interviewing you or interrogating you. I'm just talking to you." I tried not to sound too stern.

"Right, of course. Yeah. Oh. Oh my gosh, I'm just so freaked out about the whole thing. You have no idea what it's like to have one of those ... swab thingies stuck in your mouth."

And I'll keep it that way.

"Why were you touching the pizza boxes?" I asked.

Nelly's watery eyes focused on me. "I went over to help Francesca prepare for the Food Fair tasting a few nights ago," she said. "I'd been helping her a lot over the past week before the ... well, you know."

"Helping her?"

"She was struggling to keep up with the orders. You know Franny was one of the chefs at the pizzeria. Sal made her work late hours, and she'd been so upset lately, what, after finding out what she find out."

"You lost me. What did Francesca find out?" Listening to Nelly was like following the twists and turns of a white water rapid. This was what emotion did. This was why I kept it out of my investigations and my life—for the most part.

"That Sal was having an affair," she whispered. "With Bella."

"Bella." My eyebrows rose. "The friend? The long-lost friend?"

"Yes. She came here from Boston shortly after Mario, and, apparently, she hit it off with Sal. Things hadn't been right in Franny and Sal's relationship for a while, but finding out that he was cheating ... I think that was the last straw for Fran."

"She knew for sure?" I asked.

"Pretty much."

"How did she find out?"

"She never told me, she just said that it was definitely happening. She'd been unhappy for so long, I just—I told her she should get a divorce, and that she deserved better, but she never listened to me. Sal had some type of hold over her. He had her thinking that she needed him."

It sounded to me that Nelly didn't know for sure whether there was an affair going on. But it was still an interesting lead. And Bella was from Boston. From Boston, but didn't sound like she was. What did that mean?

"What do you know about Bella?" I asked.

"Not much. Just that she was a friend of

Franny's from high school, and that she moved away a long time ago."

Moved away to Boston? What had that timeline looked like? Once again, my thoughts had wandered from the current case to my mother's. I had to speak to this Bella woman the first chance I got.

"Nelly, did you tell the police this? All of this?"

"Yeah, I did. I told them everything I knew," she said, having paled at the mention of the cops again. She lifted her napkin and tore strips from it. "Do you think it's going to be all right, Christie? I'm innocent. Surely, they can't arrest me for what happened?"

I didn't want to give her false hope. "How about that milkshake?" I asked, and set to making it, without meeting her eye.

Another suspect had been added to the list. I had two incidents that now pointed toward Miss Bella Surname Unknown. It was time to take a closer look at the beauty from Boston.

14

"This type of thing makes me nervous," Grizzy said, as we parked her car outside the Russo house.

"What, driving? I know we usually walk everywhere, Griz, but you've got to give the old girl's engine a rev once in a while." I patted the dashboard of her Kia.

"You know what I mean." Grizzy unclipped her seatbelt. "Coming here under the guise of being a friendly neighbor, when really, we're here to find out if Bella decided to murder them both."

"Hmm. But would she murder Sal first? And why?" Had she flown into a rage? Poisoning by pizza, which was my assumption since there'd been no gunshots or stab wounds, didn't exactly fit the 'crime of passion' profile.

"Christie, that's not what I meant." Grizzy reached over and took the sealed pot from my lap. "I'm worried that this will come back to bite us in the butt."

The setting sun sent orange-red light streaking across the sidewalk and into the Russo's messy front yard. "I don't think they have a dog, didn't see one the last time we were here, so I think butt biting will be at a minimum."

"I mean Karma."

"Karma's a strange name for a dog." I paused, lifted a finger. "Actually, no, that's a brilliant name for a dog. Better than Curly Fries."

"Don't start with me," Grizzy replied. "Now, can we focus on the problem at hand?"

"There is no problem at hand, Griz. We're just here to be friendly Sleepy Creekers." I blinked. "I can't believe I just called myself that."

"I can't either," Griz said. "If Missi heard you she'd have a hissy fit. You, a Sleepy Creeker? In your dreams." The corners of my friend's lips turned upward.

We got out of the car and made our way up the front path. The grass hadn't been cut in weeks, it seemed, and there were faded lawn ornaments lying on their sides here and there—a withered looking gnome missing the top of his red hat, and a flamingo that didn't have a leg to stand on. Compared to the other houses in the street, the Russo's place stuck out like a tired cliché.

"What did you make, Griz?" I'd sprung the surprise visit on her at the Burger Bar this afternoon, and she'd insisted she'd have something ready to take with by this evening. Whatever it was, it smelled amazing.

"Lentil soup," she said. "It's a belly filler and even though it's not exactly a spring flavor, I thought they might appreciate the comfort food. And a break from eating pizzas."

Did anyone ever need a break from eating pizza? It sounded counter-intuitive to a happy life. But lentil soup was delicious too. Anything Grizzy made was delicious.

We tramped up the front steps, and I knocked on the door then rang the doorbell.

"I hate it when people do that," Grizzy said.

"What?"

"Both. Knock and ring. It should be one or the other."

"Shush you, or I'll do it again," I said.

The latch clacked, and the door swung inward. Bella stood on the threshold, her makeup done to perfection, and her dark glossy hair piled atop her head in a hairdo that had probably taken copious amounts of hairspray.

"Can I help you?" she asked, airily.

Yeah, no Boston accent there. If anything, it smacked slightly of New York. But faintly.

"Hi," I said, "I'm not sure if you recognize us, but we were here for the memorial service the other day. For Sal and Francesca?"

"Oh. Right." She nodded, but recognition didn't exactly spark in her expression. "What do you want?"

Tough crowd. I struggled for something to say that wasn't a command or a question or too Christie-ish.

"We came to offer our condolences," Grizzy said.

"You did that at the service, didn't you?" Bella asked.

"Yes, of course. But we know how difficult this must be for you, Bella. You're new to town, and you've lost your friend. We wanted to offer you this." Grizzy put up a smile and extended the pot. "Don't worry, it's not hot enough to burn your hands."

Bella examined the proffered pot like the lid might pop off and reveal a spider or a nest of snakes or Curly Fries. That would be my worst nightmare. Opening a pot, believing I was about to eat, only to find Curly Fries had gotten there first.

"It's lentil soup," Grizzy said.

"Thanks." Bella finally took the pot, then stood awkwardly on the front step. "I suppose you want to come in."

"Thanks," I said, ignoring Grizzy's scandalized stare.

Bella shuffled off down the hall, dragging her feet in fluffy slippers with bunny ears. She wore a black, fitted dress—different from the one she'd worn at the memorial service—and bar the slippers, seemed ready for a night out on the town.

Not that there was much to do here.

We entered a kitchen, and Bella showed us

to the kitchen table. "I don't have much time to talk," she said, and glanced past us at the kitchen door. "Mario will be back soon."

"Oh," I said. "Is that a problem?"

Bella's gaze flickered toward me as she took her seat at the table. "No. Just he needs my help with something." It seemed like a lame excuse. I didn't take it at face value.

"So," Grizzy said, "how are you holding up?"

"I'm fine. I've been better, but I'll be fine once I leave this town."

"Leave?" I asked.

"Yeah, of course. I only came to visit Fran, and now she's gone, I don't see any reason why I'd stay." Bella hadn't offered us coffee, and her attitude was still brash. Like she didn't care what we thought of her. It was a far cry from the begging and pleading I'd heard at the service.

My suspicion inched upward. Bella who had done something. Bella who wanted to leave. Bella who might have been having an affair with Sal.

"Francesca was a lovely woman," I said. "She'll be missed, greatly. And such a terrible way to go."

"Yeah." Bella glanced at the doorway again. "Thanks for stopping by, but you should leave. Mario will need my help, soon."

Griz and I exchanged a glance. There was definitely something weird going on here.

"You two are managing the pizzeria together, right?" I asked, without rising. "That must be challenging."

"No, not the pizzeria. He, uh, he wanted me to help him deal with the mice. Here. Not at the pizzeria. The pizzeria's fine."

Grizzy jerked upright and looked around. "Mice? I don't like mice. I got a cat for this exact reason."

I hinged on telling Bella that they were also good at eating dead bodies, but that might've been a step too far. "We could stay and help you if you need it," I said.

"No, thank you. The soup is more than enough. I'm sorry, but I don't feel like talking about Francesca."

"And what about Sal?" I asked, in a last ditch effort to get something, anything from this. "Did you get on well with him?"

Bella opened her mouth to answer, but the slam of the front door came. She scraped her chair back, immediately, and pointed to the back door. "Out," she said. "Now."

"What? Are you all right? Bella, is something going on that we should know about?" Grizzy asked, rising from her seat.

I got up too, the temptation to walk into the hall and see who'd entered the house nearly overwhelming me.

"No, nothing's wrong. But I don't want you here. You've overstayed your welcome, you're asking me strange questions, and I don't like it. So I'd like you to leave now, thank you."

That was that. It wasn't as if we could force her to let us stay. Grizzy and I filed out of the back door, and it slapped shut behind us. We stood on the step, shaking our heads. Grizzy went so far as to scratch hers.

"What was that about?" she whispered.

"Either she's guilty or she's scared or she's both," I said. "But we won't find out more standing here. Come on, let's go home." If we were lucky, there would be a car parked out front to clue us in on who had arrived at the house.

We picked our way through the remains of the memorial service—a toppled photo stand, Styrofoam cups, paper plates, and pieces of leftover cake. "I think we've solved the mystery of the mouse problem," I said.

When we got to the front of the house, the only car parked on the verge was Grizzy's sparkling blue Kia.

"Goose egg," I said, and peered up at the front of the house. The windows were lit, but the curtains drawn. I didn't like it. Bella had been too jumpy.

I doubted it had been because of the mice. She was up to something, and I wouldn't rest until I found out what it was.

❧ 15 ❧

Griselda had definitely outdone herself with the lentil soup. In what I could only describe as a stroke of genius, she had decided to make extra and keep some for when we got home from our failed visit to the Russo household.

The soup was divine, thick, with pieces of potato and carrot, flavored with cumin and dotted with tender shredded chicken. I gulped down another spoonful of it and licked my lips. "This is delicious, Griz. I don't know how you made lentils taste good, but it's perfect."

"Lentils are always good," Grizzy said. "And healthy for you. Nice break from the burgers."

We sat in the living room on the sofa, feasting on our soup and dipping pieces of fresh crusty bread from the bakery into it. The bread brought me to thoughts of Dolores, but I brushed them aside and tried to enjoy the soup for what it was: not another clue in a murder case.

It was great to be back in the house, now that the detectives had cleared us to live here again.

"Today was strange," Griz said. "Bella was... I didn't expect her to react that way to us being there. Francesca wasn't exactly the friendliest woman around, but she was always welcoming. I thought that a friend of hers would be similar in attitude."

I ate another spoonful of my soup.

"I wonder if Nelly knows anything about her," Griz said.

"Look who's investigating now?"

"Oh please." But Griz averted her gaze. "I'm not investigating. I'm just intrigued by the behavior, that's all. It's not a very Sleepy Creek way to act. Usually, when one brings over a treat or a gift or just a pot pie, people are nice about it. It's hospitality. It goes both ways, you know."

"No, I don't know. But I'm learning from you and this town every day."

"Don't let Missi hear you say that, she'll never let you live it down," Griz said.

"Apparently, there are a lot of thing Missi won't let me live down."

"I think I know one of them." Griz placed her empty bowl on the coffee table. Curly Fries approached from the corner, but paused at the hard stare I sent her way. She meowed and waved her tail at me.

"What's that?"

"The fact that you're interested in Liam."

"What?" I nearly dropped my bowl.

"Where is everyone getting this from? I'm not interested in him."

Grizzy gave me a look of high skepticism.

"What?" I asked.

"Oh come on, Christie, I wasn't born yesterday. It doesn't take a detective to work out that you two like each other."

"Us two?" I nearly stammered it. Not like me at all. It was past time I changed the subject.

"Yeah, you two. He's obviously got a crush on you too. Whenever you're in the room, he can barely take his eyes off you. It's sweet. It reminds me of how Arthur was with me before he asked me out on a date."

"I thought it wasn't a date," I said.

Grizzy tut-tutted. "Don't try to change the subject, Chris. You like him and he likes you. You should talk to him about that."

"I would rather get eaten alive by Curly Fries than speak to the detective about 'feelings.' I mean, really."

"It's the 21st century, Christie. Women are allowed to ask men out on dates."

"It's not so much permission I need," I replied, "as to be swallowed whole by the Earth rather than continuing this conversation." I ate the rest of my bread while Griz stared at me, shaking her head.

"You are so stubborn. Why can't you admit that you're interested in him?"

"Look, even if I was interested in him, it wouldn't matter. I'm not in Sleepy Creek to stay, remember. I've got a job to get back to after my sabbatical."

"Assuming you don't get fired for investigating."

"That's my cross to bear," I replied. "Speaking of investigating, let's get back to talking about Bella's weird behavior."

"Very smooth segue."

"I thought so." Anything beat talking about Liam. It didn't help that my stomach had birthed another billion butterflies the moment Griz had so much at hinted at him liking me. I was thirty, for heaven's sake, not eighteen. "So. You think Bella is strange, yes?"

Grizzy rolled her eyes. "I think it's weird she wanted us out of there so fast. But, I suppose, if they thought she was a suspect they would have questioned her already. Like they did with Nelly."

"How did you know about that?'

"You mean, apart from the wildfire of gossip that spread through the town the minute it happened? And the call I got from Virginia? And the second one from Missi?"

"I see your point."

"Arthur told me about it," Griz said. "He mentioned it this morning over breakfast."

"Breakfast?"

"Yeah, he helped me take Curly to the vet. She was in a terrible mood about it. Kept trying to scratch me."

"Another date so soon?" I asked.

"Anyway," Grizzy said, since it was her turn to steer the conversation away from her love life. "Arthur told me that it was a poisoning. Definitely a poisoning, but he didn't tell me what type of poison it was. Only that they found fingerprints and DNA evidence and that they were waiting for results."

"What? And you waited until now to tell me all of this?" I tucked my legs underneath myself on the sofa and turned toward her. "Arthur shouldn't be telling you any of this. That's private police business. He's jeopardizing his case."

"Well, he said that it was all information they would be releasing to the press tonight. So, not really a secret."

"Oh." I still couldn't believe it. It was unprofessional of Arthur, and if it got out, might lead to real trouble with his captain. That and she'd had the inside track on the investigation. "Next time, tell me when you get Intel like this, please."

"Intel? OK, Agent Watson." Christie laughed. "Now, can we watch some TV? I'm done with murders for now. I'd like to enjoy a sitcom."

"Seinfeld?"

"Yes, please." She got up and went to go grab her DVD boxset, leaving me in relative peace—Curly Fries hovered near the doorway, eying the empty bowls.

So, it was definitely a poisoning. But had it come from the pizza? After all, Sal and Fran had both eaten it, supposedly. But they had been ill for a while. And what DNA evidence did the cops have that might help them find the killer? Would I even be needed on this one?

Of course not.

What if Nelly had done this? She didn't fit the profile of a killer, but anything was possible.

My phone buzzed on the coffee table, and I lifted it, unlocked the screen and frowned at the text notification. I didn't get texts unless they were from Griselda.

The text was from an unknown number.

"We are watching you. Stay away from the Russo family."

My stomach dropped. Those butterflies were officially gone.

A mysterious text from the murderer? No, then it wouldn't have read 'we.' *The Somerville Spiders?* My skin crawled. I looked back at the living room window. The curtains were drawn.

I had two options: take this to Balle or investigate it myself. He'd be able to track the number, but it would also expose him to the problem, and, potentially, if there was a mole in Sleepy Creek, get back to the Somerville Spiders.

No, it was better if I took care of this myself. Assuming it was the Spiders who'd messaged me in the first place.

Another text buzzed through beneath the first. "Stay away or you'll end up like your mother."

That settled it then. The Somerville Spiders were in Sleepy Creek, and they had something to do with the Russo family.

"Are you all right?" Grizzy stood next to the DVD player. "You look like you've seen a ghost."

"I think I just have," I said, and held out my phone.

❧ 16 ☙

The pressure to figure out who'd murdered Sal and Francesca had reached fever pitch. The text I'd received last night had only made me more eager to put myself out there. I was like that —the minute somebody tried to scare me, I wanted to run right at them, ready for the challenge.

But my suspect list was still so long. The fact that the Spiders didn't want me to check out the Russo family was the first clue. Did that mean that the current Russo living there, Mario, was the main suspect?

Or had the text simply implied that I stay away from the house or the case? I couldn't assume anything until I had more information, and with nothing but a few rumors and whispers to go on—

"Chris, why don't you take a break?" Grizzy asked, and patted me on the arm.

I sat at the counter at the back of the Burger Bar, surrounded by the sumptuous smells of cooking burgers and melting cheese, the chatter from the full tables, and the occasional call from Jarvis.

I blinked at Grizzy. "Huh?"

"Take a break," she said. "You're not waiting your tables, properly, and Hedy's here to take over."

The new waitress stopped next to me, smiling. She had owlish eyes, but was a sweet girl, as far as I could tell. "Can I get a choc malt and a vanilla for those two ladies over there?" Hedy asked, gesturing to Missi and Vee, who were wrapped up in conversation.

"Yes, coming right up," Griz said.

"Thanks!" And then Hedy was off again, speeding toward another table. She was slight and good at her job and definitely a better option for a waitress than me.

"Go on, Chris. Take the rest of the day off," Grizzy said. "I know you're worried about..."

"No, no, I'm fine," I said. "The texts didn't bother me." But it was a lie. They had nudged me, thoroughly, and I thirsted to go back to the Russo house, to find out what was going on there. Perhaps, the family was connected to the Spiders somehow? What if one of the family members had been involved in my mother's murder?

"Still," Grizzy said, as she prepared the milkshakes. "Take the rest of the day off. You're more of a melancholic statue than a waitress."

I laughed and set my tray down. "Thanks, Griz. You're the best."

"No problem. I'll get Hedy or Martin to take your tables. Oh, when you get home, can you check the cupboards? I'm worried Curly's going to figure out a way past the child lock and get into the kibble." The cat was so ingenious at seeking out food, we'd taken to installing literal childproofing to the cupboards in the kitchen.

"Will do." I removed my apron and hung it up on a hook next to the kitchen doors, then waved to Jarvis and Hedy on my way out. I exited into the street and inhaled a breath of spring air. The day was full of potential, and, already, the decorations for the Spring Food Fair had started going up.

There were streamers tied to the wrought iron lampposts and a sign strung up over the street that read: ***The Sleepy Creek Annual Spring Food Fair!***

It was a happy sight, and it relaxed me a little. I doubted the Somerville Spiders and their thugs, if there were still any of them left, would leap out of the woodwork here. From my research on the gang, they had been disbanded by none other than my mother. If they were here, it wouldn't be in force. It would be some remnant of the group. Hiding, watching, and trying to scare me.

They were out of luck.

I set off down the road, tucking my hands into the pockets of my jeans. Folks nodded to me or greeted as I passed, and I returned the smiles, heading for suburbia, my mind whirring away.

Somerville Spiders. Russo. Bakery. Pizza. Poison. Where was the connection? There had to be one.

I entered the suburbs, my sneakers beating against the sidewalk, and took my hair out of its ponytail. I did it up again, absently. *I can't go home, now. No way.*

The Russo house.

Chances were, it would be empty, now, and while I wasn't about to try breaking in—

though I'd resorted to it in the past—I could still check it out.

I walked the streets of the town and approached Jackson Street. There was no need to be sneaky—I was just out for a walk—but my pulse raced, regardless, and I had to force myself not to crouch over.

The Russo house was the fifth from the corner and was as dingy as it had been yesterday evening. Weirdly, it was as if the sun had set on that house. Like it was trapped in gloom. Or maybe I was projecting because two people who'd lived there had been murdered, and I hadn't had a burger snack this morning.

I stopped across the street and stood in the shade beneath an oak. The house was quiet.

What was I doing here? It was the middle of the day, and it wasn't as if I could go snooping through the trash cans or even check out the back yard. There wasn't anything to find, but I was drawn to this place.

That stupid text.

The front door of the Russo house opened, and two figures stepped out.

I moved behind the tree and leaned casually against it, pretending, once again, to check my fingernails.

Mario, the wettest hand kisser in Ohio, stood talking to Dolores from the bakery in her polka dot cardigan. Dolores, who just so happened to have hated Sal with all her might. But how did she fit in with the Russo's? And the Spiders?

I watched out of the corner of my eye.

Dolores gave Mario a brief, platonic hug, then meandered off through the dilapidated garden and out onto the sidewalk. Mario disappeared inside the house with the slam of the screen and front doors.

I hesitated. What was Dolores doing with Mario? She hated everything to do with the pizzeria. Or had it been just Sal she'd hated? It didn't add up.

Dolores pottered across the street, patting

her fiery red hair on her head to ensure it was in the right position. Finally, she reached the other side of the road and came up the sidewalk in my direction.

I stepped into her path. "Hello, Dolores," I said. "How are you today?"

She started as if someone had goosed her. "Oh. You. Miss Watson."

"Yes, me." What was it that teary waitress had said? Rat poison? "Out for a morning walk, Dolores?"

"It's the afternoon."

"In this part of town?" I tilted my head to one side, frowning.

"I don't see how it's any of your business where I walk or when."

"Of course, not. It was just interesting, is all. You being around Sal's house. Or should I say, Mario's house? Did you come to give him your condolences?"

Dolores' mouth opened and shut. We both knew that there was no way she was interested in condolences. She'd practically thrown a party the minute Sal had passed. And Francesca was basically a two-for-one deal for her.

"It's none of your business." Dolores was surprisingly nimble. She glided by me, but it wasn't like I could stop her. What could I do? Grab her by the arm? Insist she tell me why she'd been at the Russo's place?

"Rude woman," Dolores said, over her shoulder. "You should keep your nose out of other people's business. It's not polite to pry, you know." And then she was gone, off around the corner.

I stared after her. No, it definitely wasn't polite to pry, but neither was it polite to outright murder people. And the Russo family was involved. They had to be. The itch to follow Dolores rose, but I held back.

I had a better plan. And I'd put it into action. Tonight.

The people of Sleepy Creek were surprisingly lax about security, given that they'd had four murders in their town in the span of a month. It was ridiculous, really, the ease with which I found a way into Dolores' Bakery.

The window next to the kitchen door was unlocked and cracked open. I merely had to insert my hand, unlock the door, and let myself into the dark, coolness.

Even now, the place smelled of baking cookies, buttery croissants and delicious dipping sauces. My stomach grumbled, but I ignored it. I hadn't eaten a thing since this morning.

I'd been too high energy throughout the afternoon, pacing back and forth in the living room of Griselda's house, with Curly watching me, this time, out of concern. How could I not be stressed?

The text. Dolores. The Russo family.

None of it makes sense.

That was what I was here for. Totally illegally. Because my job in Boston didn't matter in comparison to figuring out what had happened to my mother.

I crept through the dark of the kitchen, guiding myself by the glimmer of moonlight on the silver countertops. I didn't touch anything, kept a slow pace, and put my black gloved hands out just in case. Not latex, but knitted—I'd had to borrow a pair of Grizzy's, not that she knew it yet.

Grizzy was still working at the restaurant.

All the perfect excuse, the perfect timing. It was now or never.

Relax, Watson, you're not breaking out of prison or something.

I reached the kitchen door and stood next to it, easing my breaths in and out. I placed my gloved hand against the swing door and nudged it open, quietly.

The inside of the bakery was dark as well, the old timey cash register a large lump on the back counters, the trays beneath the glass display cases empty of treats. Chairs had been turned upside on tables. None of it mattered.

I exited the kitchen, slowly, searching the dark for any sign of movement, or, failing that, the flash of a beam from an alarm system. Nothing happened.

The thumping of someone moving around upstairs, along with the muffled yammer from a TV show, were the only sounds. Dolores was home, and, clearly, taking some time to relax from her busy schedule of meeting with Russo's. Potentially committing murders too.

I made my way across the interior of the bakery and stepped up behind the counter. The office door's knob was cold, even through my gloves. I turned it and entered another darkened space. This time, I'd have to risk a little light.

I shut the door quietly, brought out my cellphone and turned on the flashlight app. I directed the beam to the desk and crept toward it. If there was anything suspicious in here, I'd find it, whether it was rat poison or not.

The quiet, punctuated by the odd thump, creak or bout of laughter from upstairs, was eerie.

I set to work on the desk drawers. I rolled one open at a time and felt around, checking for false bottoms. Nothing. I moved to the filing cabinets, but they were full of folders pertaining to the bakery's finances.

"Shoot," I whispered. "Come on, there's got to be something."

If I were a murderer, where would I hide my rat poison?

If I'd been the murderer, I would have disposed of the evidence long ago. Of course, I hadn't actually expected to find rat poison here, or some admission of guilt, but there had to be evidence. I was desperate here.

What would happen if the murderer stayed in town? Another victim, perhaps even at the Food Fair this weekend?

I moved the light over the interior of the office and spotted a bookcase on the other side. I started my search, pulling out books like I expected to find a trap door to another room. Nothing, of course. This had been a blatant waste of my time.

I sighed and chased the beam over the books one last time. A leather backed journal caught my eye, and I removed it, walked it to the desk and pressed it open. Hasty writing was scrawled across the pages.

I don't see how he can think I'll ever let him get away with this.

Everyone knows he's a maniac, and that he'll do whatever it takes. What if I'm next on the list?

Tucked beneath those words, in between the pages, was a folded letter. I removed it, carefully, revealing another line of writing beneath it.

This is my evidence. If he thinks that he's going to get away with it, he's wrong. I've got all that I need to show the cops the truth. Anything happens to my bakery, and they'll know. They'll know.

I opened the note and scanned it.

You tell anyone what you saw, and you know exactly what will happen if you do. I'm watching you.

Sal.

A note from Sal to Dolores threatening her? If this wasn't a motivation for her to kill him, then I didn't know what was. Could she have been working with Mario? Or alone?

My heart leaped. I had to get this home. Get it to Liam. He would be angry at me, but what could I do? Hide the information from him? There wasn't a chance.

I slipped the note into my pocket, then walked the journal back to the bookcase and slid it into place. Perhaps, Dolores had figured hiding it in plain sight was the best option.

Quick as I could, I shifted myself out of the office and shut the door behind me, listening for noise above. All was silent now, and my breaths were too loud in my ears. I stood dead still, waiting for any sign of movement above.

It came from inside the bakery instead.

A figure moved out of the darkness to my left, in front of the counter. Tall, definitely not Dolores-sized, their face hidden in shadow.

Adrenaline rushed through my limbs, and I pushed off from the door and sprinted for the kitchen.

A throaty shout rang out, and the person thundered after me.

I wrenched the back door open and fled into the night, nearly tripped over my sneakers and caught myself on a dumpster.

The steps drew closer. A hand closed on

the back of my jacket and tugged. Whoever it was growled, and the scent of... what was that? Ketchup?

Get up! Move!

I forced myself onto my feet, but the pursuer's grip was strong. They dragged me back a step.

Take it off, Chrissy. The nickname my mother had used for me. It echoed through my mind and shocked me back to focus.

I shook my jacket off then heaved myself forward and ran down the alleyway.

The sounds of pursuit followed.

❦   18   ❦

My only saving grace was that I'd been a track star in high school. That and the fact that I'd opted not to weigh myself down with some of Jarvis' delicious burgers today.

I took corners at a speed, pumping my arms back and forth, sweat gathering beneath the woolen knit of my gloves as I pounded through the middle of town, then into the suburbs. My lungs burned, and my ears rang, but I didn't dare stop or look back.

It was a miracle whoever had been in that bakery hadn't had a gun.

I thundered around another corner, forced myself on, my breaths coming in great rasps.

Griselda's house joggled into view, the porch lights still on. A car drove past, and the old lady inside frowned at me through the windshield.

I slowed. No doubt, this would be high gossip within the next few minutes. The out-of-towner sprinting through the streets wearing all black and gloves at a quarter past eight at night.

Keep going. They might still be behind you.

I finally dared to glance over my shoulder and found the street blissfully empty of evil guys in balaclavas. Not that whoever it had been had worn one, but still. It was a relief. I was much more vulnerable without my gun and badge.

Another car drove past, another person staring out at me, and I brought myself down to a walk instead of a jog.

Almost there. Just a few more steps.

I crossed the road, stripping off my gloves as I went, the coolness washing over my skin, and opened Griselda's front gate.

Curly Fries sat on the porch, her black shape a comfort for once.

I took the steps two at a time, fished my keys out of my pocket, then unlocked the door and let myself inside. Curly followed me in, dragging her tail as she was wont to do when she had to make a choice between inside and outside, and I shut the door behind her, locked it, then latched it, then checked that I'd done both properly.

I let out a breath and sank to my butt on the floor.

"Holy dogs and cats," I whispered, between gasps.

My lungs were on fire. Jerry Lee Lewis Great Balls of Fire, fire. I huffed and puffed, then finally heaved myself up and into the kitchen. I poured myself a glass of water and glugged it down, messing some down my already sodden shirt.

Curly parked her furriness on the tiles and stared at me.

"What?" I managed. "Never seen a woman sweating before?"

Curly flicked her tail.

"Yeah, well, what do you know? You don't exactly exercise much." Talking to Curly helped. My brain was clogged with adrenaline, excitement, fear and disconnected thoughts.

I opened Griselda's not so secret candy drawer and brought out a chocolate coated nougat. I unwrapped it and shoved it into my mouth, relishing the sweetness. "Oh goodness," I muttered. "Oh my goodness."

It helped. My breathing slowed, my throat hurt from the run and the tension, but I could breathe and think again, at least. I set about making myself a pot of coffee—because this situation called for it—then sat down at the kitchen table and drew the note out of my pocket.

It was slightly crumpled, but the writing was still clear. I smoothed it out and read the note again.

A threat from Sal to Dolores. And I had been chased.

I had no choice here, I had to call the cops. Liam would likely report me to the Chief again. I'd made my bed, and I'd have to lie in it and accept responsibility for my insistence on investigating.

But for once, I had a reason for it, and it wasn't because I wanted to fast track a case. Or impress. Or find the truth as fast as possible.

It was because this was related to my mom.

"Just do it," I said.

But he'd take the note. I'd have no evidence, and a niggling in the back of my mind told me that I'd need this note in the future. That it would be important somehow, that if it involved Sal, it involved a Russo, and hadn't that text told me to stay away?

I entered Grizzy's downstairs study and used her printer-scanner combo to make a quick copy of the note. I tucked it away in my back pocket, then walked the original back into the kitchen. I poured myself a cup of coffee then made the dreaded call.

After, I changed out of my dark clothing and into something a little less suspicious.

Five minutes later, the doorbell buzzed.

Strangely, I was more nervous now than I'd been during the entire chase back to the house.

I opened the door for Detective Balle.

"Christie," he said, dapper in his uniform. "You called. Why did you call?"

I'd kept as much from him as possible on the phone to avoid the apoplectic reply. Also, I really despised making phone calls. "Come on in," I said. "We should talk."

"Why don't I like the sound of that?" He followed me into the kitchen, and we sat down at the table.

"Coffee?"

"I'll pass," he said.

I lifted the folded note from the table and handed it over to him. "I found this today."

He opened it, cast a frown in my direction, then read the note. "Where did you find this, Watson?" he asked.

"I can't tell you exactly where, but I found it."

His expression darkened. "You got involved again," he said. "Watson, you—I should arrest you for this. In fact, I have every right to. I'd be remiss not to. I'd—"

"Do it," I replied. "You're right. I shouldn't get involved, but I'm not going to stop until I figure out what's going on in this town. It's not just a few unconnected murders. It's all linked to my mother somehow."

"How can you be so sure of that?" he asked.

I nudged my phone across the table toward him. "Check my text messages," I said.

Liam did as I'd asked, then looked up at me. "Why didn't you tell me about this?" he asked. "This is a threatening message, Christie."

"Because it wouldn't have made a difference to these people. If anything, it would have made it worse. It's so clear that they want to draw me out."

"And you're letting them do that," Liam said. "You're following their trail of breadcrumbs."

"I'll do whatever I have to do to find the truth about my mother's murder." The longer I stayed in Sleepy Creek the more I realized how important it was. What had happened would stay with me for the rest of my life, unless I found a way to deal with it.

Figuring out who had done it was part of that.

"You know what a difficult position this puts me in."

"Liam, you're not the one receiving threatening messages. Quite frankly, I don't care what position this puts you in," I said.

"You're misunderstanding me, Christie. I

don't want to—" he broke off, shaking his head.

"What?"

"I don't want to get you in trouble, and I definitely don't want to see you hurt."

Heat climbed up my throat and into my cheeks. "You won't. I can handle myself."

"I don't doubt that," he said, "but these aren't the type of people you mess around with. If they are the Spiders then you need to stay out of it. You'll be their prime target after what happened to your mother. They'll want revenge."

"I know that. It's why I'm trying to stop this before any more lives are claimed."

"It's not your place to stop anything," Liam said. "It's not safe for you."

"That's what you care about?" I asked. "What about the fact that I'm interfering in your investigation?"

He massaged the bridge of his nose. "If the circumstances were different, I don't doubt I'd be asking you for help. To be a consultant on these cases since you're so closely connected with what happened here, but that can't happen. You don't have the jurisdiction or the permission to investigate here. And I've given you too many final warnings."

"What are you going to do? Call the Chief and tell him?" I asked, not in a challenging tone. Just because I needed to know what to prepare for.

I'd come to Sleepy Creek to keep my nose clean, but that hadn't happened. And it was past time I focused on figuring things out with the Spiders, even if that meant losing everything I had spent the past ten years working to build.

It was the biggest choice I'd made.

"I don't know yet," Liam said, after a minute, and his expression had softened. "I have to do the right thing. But I will have to trace this text message and find out where it came from. You should have brought this to me the minute it happened. I don't usually..."

"What?"

"I always do what's right, Christie. I put my job first, above everything else in my life. I don't have anything else. But it's difficult with you around."

"Why?"

His phone trilled in his pocket, and we both jumped. Liam brought it out, then answered it, rising as he did and walking through to the living room. "Yeah? Got it. I'll be there." He reentered the kitchen. "That was Arthur. He received a call-in to the bakery because there'd been a break-in. You wouldn't happen to know anything about that, would you?"

I shrugged.

"I'll be back for you," he said. "Try to stay out of trouble." And then he was out of the kitchen, trailing woodsy cologne. The front door shut a few seconds later.

I exhaled and rested my chin in my hand.

I had threats from every direction, but no real leads apart from the note, and even that was hearsay.

There were no options left. For the first time in a long time, I was stuck.

What now?

❧ 19 ❧

Sleep was futile.

I was alone in the house, Grizzy was still working at the Burger Bar, and every time I closed my eyes images of the past week swam back into view.

Dolores standing in front of Mario at the Russo house.

Mario smooching the back of my hand, then giving me a card.

Bella proclaiming her innocence, then shutting us out of our house without so much as a 'how do you do' the following day.

And the person in the bakery. The tall one who had chased me. I hadn't gotten a good look at the face, but the grip had been iron strong. A man or a woman? Not even the noises had given me a clue as to which it was.

"Ugh." I sat upright in bed, the sheets falling to my lap.

I'd left the curtains open, so that a sliver of moonlight could dance through and lie across my comforter, but it didn't help soothing me. Not only was a the comforter a magenta pink, but the house, old as it was, made creaking and ticking noises as it settled.

I wasn't afraid as much as I was unable to sleep because of them.

Keep telling yourself that.

Curly Fries' yellow eyes glowed at me from the comfy chair in front of the desk next to the window. She did this every night—waited until I was asleep before climbing on top of my head. No luck tonight for either of us.

I clicked on my bedside lamp, threw back the covers and clambered out. The clock read

8:45pm, way too early for me to go to bed in the first place, but I'd hope sleep would provide me with clarity.

"What?" I asked, as Curly flicked her tail at me. "I can't sleep. That's not a crime, you know." I got out of bed, walked over to her and heaved her off the chair. Heaved because she still wasn't any lighter despite the diet we'd put her on. "I'm taking you on a walk tomorrow."

I sat down at the desk, fired up my laptop and waited, tapping my fingernails on the wood.

If I could examine the evidence I did have, however slight, perhaps I could find some workable conclusion to this case.

"Let's look at the evidence," I said, and opened a word document. I wouldn't save it as that would be incriminating for me. I looked over at Curly, who had perched on top of my dresser. "Are you paying attention, cat? You're going to be my sounding board. This is very important."

To her credit, Curly didn't meow or whip her tail.

"What have we got?" I typed out a sentence. "Sal dies of poisoning. His wife, Francesca, dies two days later. Yes?" Curly blinked languidly. "Yes," I said. "Which means our murder weapon is poison. But we don't know which type of poison yet."

I launched myself out of my chair and took to pacing instead of typing. "But we do know that Dolores bought rat poison according to that crying waitress whose name I can't remember now. The Kleenex stealer. She said Dolores was mean, was happy Sal died, and had bought poison. But the cops haven't exactly investigated her or the whole town would know about it."

Curly meowed her agreement. Perhaps, it was a complaint.

"They did, however, take Nelly in for questioning. Who had left evidence at the crime scene because she was friends with Francesca. Who had been upset with both Sal and Bella because she believed Sal was having an affair. Unproven claim, but still a motive. Is it possible that Francesca killed her husband, then Bella flew into a fit of rage and killed Francesca as an act of revenge?"

But what had the note to Dolores been about? I padded to my dresser, opened it, and brought out my jeans. I rummaged around in the back pocket and extracted the letter.

I stared at the words scrawled across it. "Tell anyone what you saw? Hmmm. So, Dolores saw something. But what? Fran and Sal fighting? Bella and Sal in an embrace? And if so, why was she talking to Mario about it?"

Dolores had wanted Sal out of the picture because of the pizzeria and the Food Fair. But Mario had kept the pizzeria open after Sal's death.

And the text I'd gotten had told me to stay away from the Russo family.

I grabbed a handful of my hair and tugged. I walked over to the desk, sat down, and placed the note next to the laptop.

A note to Dolores warning her away. A message to stay away from the Russo family.

I turned to my laptop and opened up the browser, then set to researching. Both Sal and Mario were clean of criminal records, apart from what looked to be a minor misdemeanor in Mario's past—petty theft.

Bella was next. She was beautiful, a model, but clean as well.

Dolores didn't bring up any information, apart from a social media page for the bakery.

This was hopeless.

Spiders. Russo. Poison. Two dead. Bakery? Dolores. Mario inherited the pizzeria. Francesca wanted to meet with me.

Dolores and the bakery didn't seem to fit, somehow, not into the text from the gang, nor the warning, but she had been threatened herself.

I lifted the letter again, put it down.

Spiders. Russo.

I typed in the two words together, but pulled up nothing, apart from a tagged picture from another social media platform. I clicked on it.

The picture showed Sal and Mario together, their arms around each other's shoulders. They were significantly younger, too, and bore massive grins. Something about the picture called to me, but I couldn't quite place what it was.

I read the caption.

Throwback Thursday with my cousin, Sal. Never forget this day. Got my tattoo!

And underneath that was a comment from Sal himself dated a two weeks ago.

This is not a good memory, Mario. Untag me.

Why wasn't it a good memory? And a tattoo? I scanned Mario and spotted it. A small blotch on the back of his hand. My heart skipped a beat. I downloaded the photo, opened it and zoomed in. It was grainy, but the shape was there.

"It's a spider," I whispered. "It's a spider!"

Curly meowed.

It was the same tribal swirling spider I'd

seen on the back of George Brighton's hand—he had been the very first man I'd helped bring to justice in Sleepy Creek. And he had definitely been connected to my mother's murder.

My throat closed. *Think.*

"Spider tattoo. Threatening note. Mario. Mario."

He'd worn gloves at the memorial service on a warm day. Gloves to hide that tattoo.

I scrambled the desk's top drawer open and brought out the fluffy pink diary Griz had bought me as a joke. I opened it, and flipped through the pages until I found the card Mario had given me after the hand smooching.

I whipped it out, turned it over, and found the highly inappropriate message he'd scrawled on the back, just beneath his number.

Hey, sweet cheeks. Give me a call some time. Mario's here for you any time you need me.

I slapped the card down, then grabbed the

note and placed them side-by-side, scanning the strokes. They were identical. Large circles over the 'i' in place of dots. It wasn't an exact art, but it was enough. Balle had to see this.

Mario was part of the Somerville Spiders, and it was him who'd sent Dolores the threatening note, faking that he was Sal. And if that was the case, she was in grave, grave danger.

I had to get there before it was too late.

             ❧   20   ❧

I approached the bakery from the Burger
Bar's side, my heart sitting in my throat.
I didn't run in case it aroused suspicion,
or in case there was more than one Spider in
the town, waiting to leap from the shadows.

I'm not a juicy fly. They'd have a tough time
taking me down, just as they'd had a tough
time with my mother.

I slowed the closer I got to the bakery and
the antiques store next door. The lights were
on in Missi and Vee's apartment, but the
street itself was silent apart from a police

cruiser, parked out front. Either Cotton or Balle were here, at least. That was a relief.

No ambulances and just the car meant Dolores was likely fine, and that she'd obviously delayed the detectives by talking their ears off about the disturbance.

I heaved a sigh of relief, the copy of the letter I'd lifted from Dolores's office and Mario's card weighing on my mind. This would be easier than I'd anticipated. I'd be able to hand in the evidence, tell Balle what I'd found and if that somehow incriminated me, then I'd simply have to take the punishment.

The bottom line was, all the evidence I'd found so far lined up and pointed toward Mario Russo. Not Nelly Boggs. Not even Dolores, for all her gleeful celebration.

Mario who was a spider and had threatened Dolores, and Mario was the only one who had stood to benefit from Sal's death by inheriting the pizzeria.

The cold feeling in my stomach hinted at a

deeper meaning—what if the Spiders had wanted to place Mario in the pizzeria to keep an eye on me? What if Sal had seen through it and wanted him to leave? Or, perhaps, it had been Francesca who had figured it out? That would explain why she'd wanted to meet with me.

I shook my head.

Balle would know more than me, and he would be able to use this information to close the case and put the right person behind bars.

Got to be Mario. Got to be. Spider tattoo.

I stopped in front of the bakery. The lights were on inside, but the tables were empty, the chairs upside down on top of them. The office door was open—Liam sat inside, with Dolores at the desk in front of him, his notepad out. I lifted my fist to knock.

The low shuffling of something moving in the alleyway between the bakery and the antique store caught my attention.

I frowned and brought out my cellphone then strafed to the right. A figure stood in the darkness. The same tall figure that had attacked me an hour before.

What on earth were they still doing here?

"Hey!" I yelled, lifting the phone.

The person leaped from the shadows toward me, and I let out a cry, swinging my phone up to shine the light on their face. If I couldn't stop them, I could identify them, at least.

"Stop!" But the suspect hit me head on and bowled me to the ground. I fell on my side and pain screamed through my right arm. "Hey! Stop right there."

They were already off, running across the street toward the opposite side of the road.

I scrambled upright, grabbed for my phone, but found only one half of it. The other was smashed on the concrete.

No time. Go! Quick!

"Christie?" Balle spoke from the front of the bakery. "What are you—?"

"Catch them, quick!" I pointed toward the figure that was now thumping down the street at a furious pace. They dodged beneath a lamppost, and, no... it couldn't be. This didn't make any sense. The attacker had long, glossy dark hair.

I took off after her, because it was a *her*, pumping my hands back and forth, wincing every second step at the throbbing in my arm.

Balle followed me, and then he drew even with me, and then outpaced me.

"Stop right there," he shouted. "I have a weapon."

The woman skidded to a halt.

"Get your hands up." Balle drew his gun from his holster and aimed it at her back. "Behind your head. Stand still."

"I can disarm her," I said.

"No, Christie. Stay back." The detective moved forward and swiftly felt the women down for weapons. He extracted something from her pocket—a small bag that he lifted beneath the lamppost's light. It contained a fine blue powder. "Turn around."

He was well within his rights to questions

her—she'd knocked me over and had been acting suspicious right outside the bakery, which had been broken into earlier. The fact that I'd been in there too was neither here nor there.

The woman turned, and I barely kept my shock at bay.

"Bella," I breathed. "What are you doing here?"

"Nothing." She'd lost her brisk attitude.

"Christie, let me handle this." The detective grasped her by the arm. "You're coming with me, ma'am."

"No, please, I can explain. I can explain it all. Don't arrest me."

"He's not arresting you," I said. "He just wants to talk."

But Bella didn't seem to hear a word of it. She tossed her head and brought her hands down in front of her chest, clasping them together. "Please, please. I didn't kill them. I didn't kill them."

That gave both of us pause. Liam and I exchanged a glance. "Who?" I asked.

"It was Mario. He made me do it."

"Calm down, ma'am. Tell me what you're talking about." Liam guided her across the street toward the bakery. We entered it, and Liam sat the suspect down in a chair he whipped down from one of the tables.

She rocked back and forth. "I have to go. He told me I was next if I didn't put the poison in here."

"Rat poison," I said, and this time the look Liam shot my way was less than happy.

"Christie."

"I'm sorry, detective, but I came here to give you something." I brought the card out of my pocket then the copy of the letter I'd made. He studied them both. "See? They're the same. Mario wrote the note to Dolores."

Bella let out a choked cry. "He's evil," she whispered. "He made me do this."

"Do what?" the detective asked.

"Is everything all right?" Dolores the baker stepped out of the office, her polka dot robe clutched tight to her chest. "Detective?"

"Everything's fine, Ms. Baker."

"But—"

"It was Mario!" Bella's howl came over the start of Dolores's sentence. "He told me if I didn't put poison in Dolores' coffee grounds, he would kill me. He told me that he would never let me go. He said I stole from the Spiders."

My heart *tha-thumped*.

"The Spiders." The detective's gaze danced from Bella to me.

"Yes, he's one of them. He thought I was stealing from the pizzeria but I—" She burst into tears. "I couldn't do it," Bella said, between sobs. "I couldn't poison the coffee grounds."

"My heavens." Dolores trembled on the spot. She backpedaled and nearly tripped over one of the tables. I hurried to her side and kept her upright.

"Where's Mario?" Detective Balle asked.

"He's back at the house," Bella managed.

Within the span of the five minutes, Balle had the ambulance, Arthur Cotton and a team of police officers, and the rest of the town all down at the bakery. He rushed off into the night, and I couldn't follow, not with Dolores leaning on me, faint.

I had been right, though there hadn't been too much evidence pointing to him. Just the tattoo, and the poison. Of course, Bella had mentioned a mouse problem at the Russo house, and she'd been so insistent that we use the backdoor to leave when Mario got home.

Still, it didn't answer all of my questions.

Mario was guilty. But why? Why had he killed his cousin?

❧   2 1   ❧

Rumors about Mario and what had
happened were rife, even on the day
of Sleepy Creek's Annual Spring
Food Fair. Folks could barely talk about anything else around their burgers or their treats,
or between sniffing flowers or buying trinkets.
The out-of-towners who came in for the fair
wound up getting involved in the gossip too.

I helped serve burgers and ring up orders
at our stall across from the fountain, my gaze
occasionally moving over to Dolores' stand,
which was doing a roaring trade after the town

had discovered that, yes, she had nearly been killed. And by a mobster no less.

"Here's your change," I said, and handed it to the woman who'd ordered two chicken burgers from me. "Thank you for your patronage." Thankfully, my arm hadn't been damaged from the fall. Just bruised.

She disappeared into the crowd and the next customer came forward. Or rather, the next two customers.

Missi and Vee both wore a sun hat a piece. Missi's was too floppy for her head, and she flicked the end of it, now and again, growling at the way it sagged over her eyes.

"Ridiculous," she said. "Shouldn't have let you talk me into this hat."

"Oh, please, Mississippi," Vee said. "It's a lovely sunny day. It's imperative we protect our skins."

"Morning, you two. Chicken burgers?"

"Four please," Vee said, and brought out her money purse. "Murder makes us hungry. Or rather, resolved murders."

"Mario." Missi said his name like he was a harbinger of the apocalypse. "Rumor has it he killed Sal for the money from the pizzeria. And then when Fran figured it out." Missi drew her finger across her throat. "Offed her too. Horrible creature. I'm glad that handsome detective of yours put him behind bars."

I hurriedly put in Missi and Vee's order, then collected two readymade burgers from the waiting stack that Jarvis had piled at the end of his production line. I handed them over, accepted the money and gave them their change.

"Thank you for your patronage," I said.

The women hurried off muttering to each other, Missi occasionally flicking the front of her floppy hat. They wore matching flowery dresses and took their burgers to the very same bench Griz and I had sat on at the start of this week.

"Hey." The deep voice of the next customer sent a shiver done my spine. Not an entirely unpleasant one, either.

"Hello, detective," I said, as calmly as I could manage.

Liam was out of uniform today. He wore a white cotton t-shirt that fit him too well for my liking, and a pair of blue jeans. He had done his dark hair to one side. His chin dimple was ridiculously attractive, too.

"Do you have a moment?" he asked. "It's important."

"Hedy?" I beckoned to our waiting assistant. "Would you mind taking over for a while?"

"Sure, no problem, Miss Watson," Hedy said, dipping her head.

"Call me Christie."

"Of course." Hedy slipped into place in front of the cash box, and Liam moved around the side of the stall.

I walked to the back of it, stripping off my apron as I went. As vain as it seemed, I didn't want to have this conversation with Liam while I was ketchup stained. Besides, it was always better to look good when receiving bad news.

We walked off between the stalls to a quiet spot between the trees and stood underneath a maple. Its fiery red leaves bobbed in the spring breeze, and the distant tinkle of laughter traveled from the stalls.

"Nice day," he said.

"Are you here to arrest me?" I asked.

"What? No." Liam laughed. "Why do you ask?"

"I thought... after finding that note. You know?" He didn't know exactly how I'd gotten my hands on that note, only that I had. He saw it as interfering. He was right, but I wasn't about to tell him that.

"No, Christie, I'm not here to arrest you. I have no proof that you interfered in the case. No one has told me anything. The only person who's acting suspicious is Nelly Boggs. She keeps singing your praises, talking about how you single-handedly brought down a dangerous killer."

"Technically, he brought himself down. Messy death. Easy leads to follow," I said, then cleared my throat. "I mean, from an outside perspective, that's how it seemed. So, Mario's behind bars?"

"Yes. He appears to have murdered Sal for his money. He planned on selling the pizzeria."

"And the Spiders?"

"He won't say anything about them. Maintains that the tattoo is nothing but a tattoo, and that he's not part of any gangs. He lawyered up the minute I pressed harder." Liam shook his head. "There I go again, telling you things I shouldn't. It's easy to talk to you. Feels like I'm talking to my partner. Arthur I mean. Partner Arthur."

"So, Mario is pretending he's not a Spider, and that he killed Sal and Francesca for money."

"Francesca found out what had happened after the fact."

"And Bella was a tool he used to silence

Dolores because she had seen... what?" I asked. "That part doesn't make sense to me."

Liam sighed. Perhaps, he realized that I wouldn't be satisfied until we discussed this. "Because Dolores witnessed him stealing poison from the hardware store. She was too afraid to come forward for the fear that she was next on Mario's list."

"Afraid, but still celebrating Sal's death like it was Christmas."

"The enigma of Sleepy Creek's residents," Liam said.

We both chuckled, awkwardly.

"So, wait, you're not here to arrest me?"

"No," Liam said.

"And you're not going to report me to the Chief?"

Liam's smile broadened. "What for? It's not like you did anything wrong. You just got a text and found a note. That phone number that sent you the text was a burner, by the way. Couldn't trace it."

"Oh." I tucked my hands into the front

pockets of my jeans. "That's fine." What else could I say? Mario might've lied about his spider tattoo, but I knew the truth. The gang, or at least some of their members, were still alive and kicking around. And they had come to Sleepy Creek.

For me.

"Wait," I said, looking up at Liam. "If you're not here to arrest me or tell me you reported me then why are you here?"

Liam scuffed his shoe against the grass, looked down at me, his caramel colored eyes glowing. "I wondered if maybe you'd like to grab a cup of coffee sometime."

"You, what?" It didn't compute. "What do you mean? Do you need to consult with me about something?"

"No, Christie," he said. "I meant on a date. Would you like to go on a date with me?"

"Huh?" I licked my lips. "I mean, yes. Yeah, sure. That would be fine. Of course, yeah." *Stop talking, right now.* I snapped my mouth shut.

"Good. Then, I'll call you sometime. We can go grab a coffee. Sound good?"

"Sure." I tried to affect that cool as a cucumber attitude. It didn't come naturally. I was suddenly aware of my arms and how weird they felt hanging at my sides.

"Great," he said. "I'll see you around, Christie."

"Sure." Was it the only word left in my vocabulary?

Liam gave me one last grin then walked off, heading back between the stalls and toward the path that led past the fountain. I stared after him, my heart pounding away. It was the fastest it had beat in a long time.

"There you are!" Grizzy stepped into view, her apron streaked with ketchup, a smear of mustard on her cheek. "Come quick. There's been an emergency."

"Condiment related?" I asked, unable to keep my lips from bending into a smile.

"What does it look like?" Griz paused.

"Wait a minute. What are you so happy about?"

"Nothing," I said, and laughed. "Nothing at all."

Perhaps, living in Sleepy Creek wasn't such a bad thing after all. Sure, there were murderers, and, potentially, the remnants of a disbanded gang of mobsters were on my tail, and Curly Fries occasionally tried to suffocate me in my sleep, but it had its good points.

The burgers, the friends, the funny times, and, of course, the handsome detective.

I followed Grizzy back to the stall, my stomach bubbling with excitement for what tomorrow would bring.

Christie's adventures continue in *The Breakfast Burger Murder.* You can get it here!

CRAVING MORE COZY
MYSTERY?

If you had fun with Christie, you'll want to meet Milly and her pet bunny Waffle. You can read the first chapter of Milly's story below!

"It's unheard of! A travesty." My grandmother, Cecelia Pepper, sat on the edge of her seat at the coffee bar in the Starlight Cafe. "Why, the sheriff ought to be ashamed of himself. How are we meant to walk down the streets in this town with this... threat in the backs of our minds? Looming! Like some giant Sword of

Damocles over our heads." She tapped the newspaper, a copy of *The Star Lake Gazette*, she'd laid on the coffee bar the minute she'd sat down.

My grandmother was the definition of dynamite in a small package. At 75-years-old, she was brimming with vigor to make up for her height.

"I'm sure Sheriff Rogers will figure it out." I fixed Gran a cup of coffee—a hazelnut latte with extra cream—and placed it in front of her. "It's a small town, Gran. They'll catch whoever's doing this."

"A small town that's going downhill quickly." My grandmother glanced around as if she was afraid of someone overhearing our conversation.

But the painful truth was there was nobody in my cafe this morning. Just like there'd been nobody in it the day before.

As I'd learned quickly, folks in Star Lake, Iowa, were insular. They didn't care that my late father, a town favorite, had left me the cafe. I hadn't lived in town long enough for them to trust me, and then there was the fact that I had absolutely no experience in the hospitality industry.

Not now. Just take a breath and smile.

"I mean, really. A mugger? Here? Nancy from the bakery told me her sister's best friend's cousin was attacked. Wallet stolen. Can you believe that? If I didn't love the lake and the people so much," my grandmother continued, lifting the latte, "I'd move away in a heartbeat."

"Gran."

"I'm serious."

"Gran, you've lived here for thirty-five years."

"Fine. I might not move, but I'll protest this at the next town council meeting. You can mark my words on that." Gran took a sip of her latte, pressed her lips together and fluttered her eyelashes. "Nearly as good as your father used to make."

A silence ensued, filled with our shared

sorrow. It was too soon to talk about him.

I cast my gaze away from Gran and studied the interior of the cafe. Light streamed through the windows and the glass front doors, illuminating the linoleum that was in need of a revamp, as well as the checked tablecloths and laminated menus. The chairs were comfortable and well worn. The cash register was an antique and the walls were dark wood.

Overall, the aesthetic was typical of my dad's taste. Hastily thrown together but with plenty of heart.

"This really is good." Gran must've noticed the lump in my throat. Metaphorically, of course. "You know, you'll make a fine restaurant owner. As fine an owner as you would've made a detective."

That was another touchy subject. "Thanks, Gran." I forced a smile.

She reached over and patted my forearm.

Movement outside on the brick-paved sidewalk caught my attention. A homeless woman, wearing a shabby coat and carrying several plastic bags, walked up and took a seat outside the cafe.

"Oh dear," Gran said.

"Do you know her?"

"Only by sight," Gran replied. "She's new to town I think. I'm not familiar with her story. Poor woman."

I bit down on my lip then headed back to the coffee machine and started fixing another latte. Much to my surprise, the bell over the door tinkled, and Sheriff Rogers entered.

He was in his late fifties, with a gray mustache, balding, and wearing his uniform with pride. He sauntered over to the bar and eyed me. "Morning."

"Good morning, Sheriff," I said. "What can I get for you today?"

The sheriff didn't immediately answer me. He scanned the interior of the cafe then pointed over to a new section I'd set up, with the help of my cook, Francesca. "What's that?"

"That's the waffle station," I said, smiling. "Do you want to try it out? We prepare the waffles fresh, bring 'em out to you, and then you decorate them as you see fit. There's ice cream and maple syrup, there's—"

"That wasn't here when Frank was running the place."

"No," I said. "No, it wasn't. I figured that people would enjoy—"

"Waffles?"

"Sheriff Rogers," my grandmother said, and the sheriff jumped a little.

"Celia." He sniffed, using Gran's nickname. "Shoot. I didn't see you there." And he sounded truly regretful, like he was anticipating a volley of complaints. He wouldn't have been wrong in that respect.

"What's this I hear about a mugger?" Gran tapped the newspaper. "A mugger in our midst?"

"Well, yeah, there have been reports of muggings over the past week, but I assure you it's under control."

"Now, Sheriff, you know better than to shovel that level of manure around me," Gran said. "I want answers, and I want them now. What am I supposed to tell the ladies in my book club? That we can't walk to the library in peace?"

"I assure you..."

The conversation faded out as I finished off the latte, grabbed a cupcake from the display of about a dozen under the glass counter, and walked out into the sunlight.

It was the end of summer, the weather a temperate 70 degrees with a soft breeze brushing down the street. I stopped in front of the homeless woman.

"Good morning," I said.

She glared at me, her skin tan, and her ire obvious. "What do you want, Red?"

The urge to brush my fingers through my red hair nearly overtook me. Thankfully, my hands were full. "Uh."

"Let me guess. You want me to move. It's a free country, you know, I—"

"No," I said. "I just wanted to check if you were OK."

"OK?"

"Yeah." I handed her the coffee and the cupcake. "You need anything?" It was my experience, after working as a beat cop in the city, that everyone had a story. Just like everyone had a purpose. Sometimes life just... got in the way.

The woman blinked. "Uh. Yeah. I'm good. Thanks."

"Sure. Just holler if you need a glass of water or something," I said. "I'll be inside."

The woman, still full of mistrust, nodded then took a sip of her coffee. I headed back into the cafe and found Gran and Sheriff Rogers embroiled in their argument.

"—muggers on the streets. If you think that we'll stand for this then you're delusional. You know, I can call up the heads of the three factions, right now, and get them to arrange a meeting."

Sheriff Rogers, blustery as he was, paled at that.

The "factions" as they were called, were the three unions that pretty much ran Star Lake. There were "the boaters", "the butchers", and "the bakers"—and they frequently disagreed on issues, to the point where the town was practically split into three. It was expected that you'd fall into line with one of the groups even if you weren't an active member of said union.

"The bakers would be most interested to hear about your lack of action when it comes to crime on our streets. I mean, this whole area is packed with bakeries and restaurants. This is bound to affect tourism too. And then the boaters will get antsy."

The summer months in Star Lake were famed for their fun boating activities, from tours on the lake, to fishing, to jet skiing and recreational activities.

"You're complaining about mugging and crime on the street," Sheriff Rogers said, finding his voice, "yet you won't stop your granddaughter over here from feeding said criminals."

Gran jerked back as if she'd been slapped—a strange effect on a tiny woman in a floral-print dress. "Feeding them? I think the heat is getting to you, Sheriff."

"She just took out a coffee and a cupcake to..." He trailed off and gestured toward the homeless woman now sitting on a bench out front.

"And so?" Gran grew red and rose from her barstool, trying to tower at four feet eight inches.

The sheriff tugged on his collar. "All I'm saying is that if you don't want trouble, don't invite it into your home." And with that, he swept from the cafe, trailing his overbearing spicy cologne.

"Idiot," Gran muttered.

"Gran."

"There's no love lost between us." She resumed her seat. "And for good reason."

But she didn't go into the reason. I fixed a cup of coffee for Francesca, who was in the kitchen, patiently awaiting orders that would likely never come, and then joined my grandmother at the counter.

Gran paged through the newspaper, stopping on an image and tapping it. "See, now, this is why you don't want to get on the wrong side of those boaters. Look at that. A full page ad for their 'Boating Blowout 2021.'"

I read over her shoulder. "Join us for a boating extravaganza as we celebrate the end of summer."

"You're going, I assume? Everyone's going," Gran said. "Everybody who's anybody. It will be a great opportunity for you to network, dear. It's been a year, and you've only made one friend."

"Thanks, Gran."

"I'm just saying," she replied, "that it might be a good opportunity for you to get out there and meet someone."

"Meet someone? The only person I'm interested in meeting is an accountant who can help me manage my finances for this place." Things were *not* looking good. And I was *not* about to let down my father's legacy by losing the Starlight Cafe.

"I'm sure there are plenty of eligible accountants around."

"Not what I meant, Gran."

She gave me a sneaky smile, and it cheered me up. I couldn't stay mad at Gran.

"Are you coming by tonight for supper?" Gran asked. "I'm making chicken casserole. You can bring Waffle along."

"That sounds great."

It sure beat eating a microwave dinner over the kitchen sink.

Want to read more? You can grab **the first book** on all major retailers.

Happy reading, friend!

Macarons and Murder

Candy Cake Murder

Murder by Rainbow Cake

<u>*A Milly Pepper Mystery series*</u>

Maple Drizzle Murder

<u>*A Sunny Side Up Cozy Mystery series*</u>

Murder Over Easy

Muffin But Murder

Chicken Murder Soup

Murderoni and Cheese

Lemon Murder Pie

<u>*A Gossip Cozy Mystery series*</u>

The Case of the Waffling Warrants

The Case of the Key Lime Crimes

<u>*A Mission Inn-possible Cozy Mystery series*</u>

Vanilla Vendetta

Strawberry Sin

Cocoa Conviction

Mint Murder

Raspberry Revenge

Chocolate Chills

<u>*A Very Murder Christmas series*</u>

Dachshund Through the Snow

Owl Be Home for Christmas